Ireland
I Don't Recognise
Who She Is

Ireland
I Don't Recognise
Who She Is

JAMES TUNNEY

ISBN: 9781072957270

To My Seven Sisters

'Ah, the Neon Mile. Where value wears a neon sombrero and there's not a single church or library to offend the eye.'

Homer Simpson, Treehouse of Horror VI

'The sciences, each straining in its own direction, have hitherto harmed us little; but some day the piecing together of dissociated knowledge will open up such terrifying vistas of reality, and of our frightful position therein, that we shall either go mad from the revelation or flee from the deadly light into the peace and safety of a new dark age.'

Lovecraft, The Call of Cthulhu

'A coward dies a thousand times before his death but the valiant taste of death but once.'

Shakespeare, Julius Caesar

'Just because you got the monkey off your back, does not mean the circus has left town.'

George Carlin

'O wise men riddle me this: what if the dream come true?

What if the dream come true? and if millions unborn shall dwell in the house that I shaped in my heart…'

Padraig Pearse, The Fool

'Go, go, go beyond, go thoroughly beyond, and establish yourself in enlightenment.'

Dalai Lama

'The eversower of the seeds of light to the cowld owld sowls that are in the domnatory of Defmut after the night of the carrying of the word of the Nuahs and the night of making Mehs to cuddle up in a coddlepot, Pu Nuseht, lord of risings in the yonderworld of Ntamplin, tohp triumphant, speaketh.'

James Joyce, Finnegans Wake

'**Future** (n.) That period of time in which our affairs prosper, our friends are true and our happiness is assured.'

Ambrose Bierce, The Devil's Dictionary

'When a man cannot choose, he ceases to be a man.'

Anthony Burgess, A Clockwork Orange

'My primary vision was of a conflict constant in history found, e.g., in the book of Daniel in which an enslaved people fight against a tyrannical empire to establish a just empire under messianic rule....... This, simply, is because the Empire is back and stronger and worse than ever.'

Philip K. Dick, The Exegesis of Philip K Dick

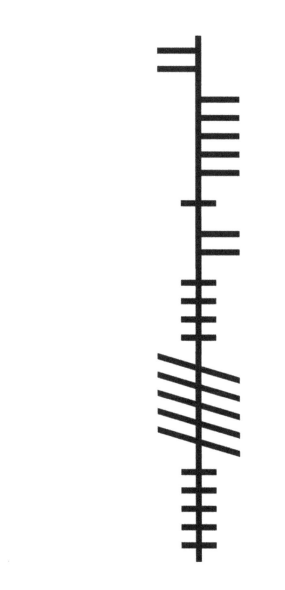

POD137
DUBH DÓITE

Day's dead, all flame-bewildered, and the hills
In list'ning silence gazing on our grief.
Yeats

Cullen was sick. He was always sick. Sick was normal. Not just in the body but in every way, SURFs were never very well. Just well enough to work. Some were podded so bodily fluids could be siphoned off from them while they slept a very long sleep. HIKs. Electromagnetic energy was also somehow extracted. It was so normal to be ailing that you forgot you were ill. It just meant that sometimes before he began his shift, he might find it hard to get up from his pod. Starvelings lag all the time. If he did not rise, then the severest consequences would follow. One day he would be too frail to rise. Then you were gone. When you were debilitated you had to be careful that the suction unit for the bodily waste did not draw in parts of your body. Turned inside out. Then you would be beyond recovery. When you live in a mist of incomprehension, where your bearings have been taken away and your minimalistic life-force is a mere trickle, the next step in your monotonous tasks takes all your will-power. You are far beyond the pale of meaning. Far beyond the fire of love. Beyond the comfort of conviviality. The mercy of forgiveness. Balm of concern. Then there was the problem of thinking. First, they take your space to think. Then they take your words. Then they take the chance to talk. All the while they sucked meaning like vampires. Then the thing in your head imploded so there was nothing else to do but focus on getting by. Just about. Fragile. Existing. I'll go on. Why go on? It was hard to think what to do. What you should do. He got up out of the grubby plastic, multi-coloured, coffin-like bunk that was home when he was not working, not doing whatever he was told to do. Slaves do what they are told. He rose and struggled out into the turquoise twilight to make his way to work. But even his weary walk would be made worse. Though he was often on the fringe of nausea he somehow would not alter his old human state to the Sapiens-beings around, even if he had the chance. Even if the disorientating control mechanisms meant he could not think straight and must accept external electronic inputs from the matrix, he was still human. The cyborgs that were human once upon a time could do wondrous things but he was glad he was not evolving. Low homo sapiens would do him still. Even if he had no choice but to eat the spiky insectmash or factoryhumanflesh and perish for lack of machine inputs. The once unimaginable were normal now and the once ordinary were 'sub-normals.' Those who did not embrace all the implants, enhancements, adaptations were 'unevolving' feeble decreps and beneath contempt only fit to serve the enlightened adapters. All the weird dreams of the lonely fantasists had been realised in a wearied, wired, wyrd world. With great difficulty he rose.

THE ISLAND. A HAMMOCK HEMLÄNGTAN

Birgitta watched her two laughing sons play and contest on the sifted sandy beach from the deep greenshade under the palm tree while rollers broke on the white sand with regular smooth swooshes. Cool meditation. Cool, fresh coast. Calm escape from the tall roasting sun. They were growing up fast here in this tropical heat. Thankfully removed from the madness without. What the future held, nobody could tell. All she knew was that she had done one other good thing apart from having her family and coming here away from the disorder. She saw her grandmother in her mind's eye in her lush little garden in Sweden before it had all gone sour. A time ago. The air was precious with perfume of plants and bees flew dazed and drunkenly from blossoms hung heavy all around the blue wooden house. She saw her happily move between the growing things and profusion in the heat of summer. In her mind she could see her too in spring when mormor showed her how to plant things. She remembered with her own small hands putting a seed down in the moist, brown ground and patting the soil over it and wondering why it was buried so, whether it had died. Then later she understood. That little lesson was a blessing beyond the seemingly simple procedure that we take for granted. She herself would look out the leafy window standing on pale planks sipping saft and nibbling cinnamon and ginger homemade biscuits, in case anything might happen. A miracle of one world inscribed in another little carrier, compressing all the past and the possible futures in a converged compact or code like a betting chip at a casino that may win a million or make you bust. Butterflies would like them when they come up she said. When it is time. She told her of such things and morfar told how the pearls in her necklace formed. Other seasons too. Blueberry time, golden yellow, red leaves of autumn and mushrooms, chestnut time, snow time, red cheeks, skating, homely flickering flames in winter. Maybe it was time to cool down now. Take a dip in the deep blue cooling tide. Feel the mane of seaspray on your body. That lesson of long ago, in a faraway place, obviously registered in a deeper way. Paradise is peripatetic. So is hell. Thankfully, it was not here... yet. Sweeping power surf swashing the foreshore seen separating two dimensions in the horseshoe bay so seeming to seep into your spirit to cleanse to clean to swish on powdered sand to swat away the senses I have no wish to retain today. When the lepidopterists came to enchanted places like this to net blue and green beauties for Science and Lord Rothschild and preserve them, they prefigured that nasty but convincing novel *The Collector* and probably suggested how the majesty of our consciousness would be pinned down in some eternal prison for the satisfaction of some psychopaths or obsessives primed with some objective reason.

BAY AREA. WESTRON WYNDE WHEN WYLT THOU BLOW SUAIMHNEAS

A pity beyond all telling
Is hid in the heart of love:
Yeats

One might not know what another thinks or how they do, even if the likely lineaments of mental landscapes seem apparent. Collectivisation of individual consciousness made some aware of its preciousness in a way hitherto unappreciated. That yielded was the essence impossible to achieve when the drop was subsumed in the ocean. Would that I could have that tender individual sense however adulterated existence renders it. The force may be with you but that is not the end of it. Had hoped that it might be experienced really in some manner. The peace that passeth understanding was one thing. There were also poles of satiation or emptiness. A time to be joyous, a time to be ecstatic. Not that. It was not a general sense of tranquility that was yearned for. It was neither a peak nor a plateau. In many ways, it seemed to be something more transient and fleeting. Within that fleetingness there seemed to be a sense that everything was well. It need not be the towering mystical state of unity with the cosmos, it was altogether more modest but nevertheless more worthwhile in a way, in its ordinariness and familiarity. If you were lucky enough once upon a time you may have got it with people you know. It may have been in the distant past when you were a child or watching a child play and being happy in the moment of forever. But it was often something unexpected and sneaking catching you unawares. It caught your attention like a cat catches a mouse and flings it in the air. Perhaps the sudden sight of cherry blossom clusters or a suddenly sprung lilac. A field brightly buzzing hazy early summer golden. Wafting sense in the air, maybe a scent of lavender, a squelch of healing, warm oil to be spread on the stretched skin parched. Water tinkling down sparkling on a sunny day with an inkling of eternity. A boat in the spray of a blue afternoon. Snow falling faintly and softly to relieve a heavy sky. Susurrations. Wild flowers. Woodpecker. Deer shyly seen straying in wooddim light. Not even so dramatic. Lesser but more. Something small that seems to lift the weight of the world away so you might perceive a moment of peace. A sound, a bell, a chime, a rhyme. Not even the winding Milky Way nor the pulsating Northern Lights. Starlight yes. A swallow or a swift on an early summer's late lighted eve. Or watching them return under the eaves to share the blue summer, leaving the parched lands for the light-blossomed air. Just a nice, sense of belonging in peace. Once upon a time the world was like that, if you can believe it or not. The Universe is meant to be bliss. Consciousness insufflates into people. It is undivided before. We drink a draught of forgetfulness when we come in but the soil is there to grow fresh. But through the veils of illusion the beauty of the world that will pass will perchance penetrate the paths of the senses to stir the permanent heart that is us. I shift my focus. I seek to grow. I seek to know myself. I may have something in me that should not be there. I see he comes to me.

BOROBUDUR. JAVA. ZONE 3
FAOI THALAMH

The fascination of what's difficult
Has dried the sap out of my veins,
Yeats

In 1814 Sir Thomas Stamford Raffles had been involved in facilitating the recovery of the great Borobodur Temple from the jungle and volcanic ash. It was not plain sailing then. There had been exploitation of the stones. The religious composition of the people had changed. This had been a land of Ancestor Worship, Hinduism, Buddhism and then Islam. The Dutch and British had intervened and shaped it somewhat. The East India Company with its love of the opium trade and exotic things like spices, sugar, silver, copper and tin, was the vessel and the Napoleonic Wars the context. Felix stood and surveyed the jungle and hills round the grey monument well over a thousand years old with thousands of carvings. He felt that damp odour of the East that he loved. It was something to savour before the strong sun took your mind off it. He was unsure why he felt compelled to visit this place. Soon it would be buried once again. Superstition had no place in the New World. At least they were not bulldozing it like many others. Maybe the biggest Buddhist monument in the whole world. Mentioning The Buddha was not something you should do in polite company. For some reason, unlike most of his colleagues, he thought it was a bad idea to bury it. The world got a little duller for him with the permanent revolution that razed everything down to the ground that could not be justified by the god of the Objectives. He knew it was 'scientific' to remove superstitious things associated with the supernatural. He knew it was reasonable, rational, objective, consistent with evolution. There was nothing else. He enjoyed the sparkling air, the majestic panorama, the deep, green sense of the place around the grey stone. The genius of another people. The wisikan, the whispering wind. Sirna, vanished. Widik, widik, that which is seen or heard but not known, as thunder. Then súnya, solitude. Something you have an idea of but cannot see clearly like the sky, lang'it. We are good at making kunjára. Places of confinement. Science is one admirable thing. Reason one admirable tool. But the soft, incessant power of the steady dripping streamwater of spirit from ordinary people in their accommodation with an enchanted environment, wears incomprehension away in a way that science's brutal breaking and bullish crushing can never seem to do. The price of benefits are high and the tone and tenor of those wrenching techniques seep alas inevitably into the disenchanted domain created in its wake. Even within the keep of the heart so that no finer care is kept there crept the cold displacement force. He longed for something, maybe a deep friendship, even love. But where? Machines lack some empathy however good they are at mimicking it.

THRESHOLD OF THE GRAND LUMINOSITY. CARCOSA BANBA TROMLUÍ

The blood-dimmed tide is loosed, and everywhere
The ceremony of innocence is drowned;
Yeats

You think you are leading your life and then you realise there is an invisible halter around your neck. The force can go two ways, the right way or the wrong way. It can follow the line of integration or move down the line of disintegration. You're going the wrong way. No doubt Neanderthals enjoyed life and wanted to persist. Who lost sleep over them? Then they brought them back as pets, curiosities in those gene-zoos they have. They had forgotten about the human zoos in the 20th century and people did not anticipate that they would come back with some of them in them. Menageries of gene armies in the risen me age. The tragedy of the tragedy of history is the tendency to forget that tragedy or assume the impossibility of its recurrence and indeed potential increase. Irony only works when things go against expectations. As the world became unpredictable and perverse the previously ironic twist became the cord of truth. Reason somehow made things unreasonable. Every front has a back. If Adam and Eve is myth, why could it not be a warning about the metaphorical beginning of the end? The time when primacy of spirit was taken away in the pursuit of knowledge. This message is for you. My last I am sure. That place is more like a hope for me. You may feel good when you signal your virtue in meaningless clichés but that only feeds the rough slouching beast now born, alas. I, nor anyone else knows how it will go. I am here to warn you. Yes you. I look through the keyhole in the asylum but from the freer side. You may not believe my message is for you but it is. Prepare a wreath or rather kneel and say an Ave there... wait you gave that up, not for me, though I could do with it, but for you all. Not just for the people of the Island of the Woods or the Noble Island, as it once was but is no longer, but for most, save the ones who are responsible. That would take forgiveness beyond any realms of meaning or comprehensibility. The same story is afoot across the globe. You might fear a terror that lasted 28 years, how heavy is eternity then? I am not sure whether it is Carcosa in Banba where you see it most clearly despite the dense, dank mist. Who is behind this? This is but one question. But it is not the most important one. Even if one conceded that an intelligence superior to our own scrutinised us, it would not be the end of it. Wells forewarned us because he knew what this was going to be, but disguised the identity.

> *'With infinite complacency men went to and fro over this globe about their little affairs, serene in their assurance of their empire over matter. It is possible that the infusoria under the microscope do the same.... Yet across the gulf... minds that are to our minds as ours are to those of the beasts that perish, intellects vast and cool and unsympathetic, regarded this earth with envious eyes, and slowly and surely drew their plans against us.'*

Empire of matter mattered critically. Whatever cause is truly there, it is clear that the evolution of the tangible, material world changed it. Despite the great boons, consider this. There seems to be a direct relationship between the rise of the love of material things, machines, matter and the demise of the love of immaterial things. Unfortunately, those immaterial things were the special unique heritage of all humankind. Myth, story, numinosity, culture and spirit. It was not that you were made of such stuff as dreams are made on, it was much grander than that. As the things became all that matter, the non-matter was ridiculed as a relic. To sleep perchance to dream and there's the rub. Wells knew the watchers were not on Mars but were around with his ilk. You are nearly in Carcosa. You might be there already. I warn you and I may condemn you for this. Even though it could be someone like me who sends you there, if you are not already destined. Maybe some have a certain delight in watching the helpless become the hopeless despite their warning to those who had the choice. You send so many to Coventry but you end up in Ca… you know where… in one form or another. There was no delirium that struck your psyche such that you would have no power of election. It was not right nor left, it was both right and left. But most of all it was behind and beyond all that. Beyond. You let them take away things bit by bit. It was a shapeshifter. It is you who have ceded and conceded in your conceit for curios and baubles. If even I can see that, you can. I mean this with the respect of someone who urges another not to proceed on their next step, because unbeknownst to them they will step over a precipice. You might have been led to think that a terrible death would be to be eaten say by a great white shark in one bite or to disintegrate in an explosion and thus not to be. But they have the benefit of being mercifully quick and, even if your body realised, it would be too swift to feel much. What you should fear more is a slow, lingering loss of sovereign consciousness, not physical disintegration but moral and spiritual leakage and existence in your dispirited state, maybe in a brainfarm for millennia or on some inescapable computer for eternity. Hemingway said that Shakespeare was wrong and that the brave die two thousand times but don't mention it. The price of Them wanting to live in The Land of Eternal Youth is your eternal slavery. Was it for this the sons of Róisin shed their blood? This is beyond nations now. Luke Kelly angrily got it.

'FOR WHAT DIED THE SONS OF RÓISIN…'

Rage, rage against the dying or the daily diminution or your spiritual light. You There! You... you... yo... ou... o... u… dare... you…. are... you... there… uu… To whom do… we… owe… our allegiance….today..? I feel as if there were some grit creating a pearl within my tender thoughts.

ZONE 7. KASTEL X
OUTSIDE SURFQ
TAIRSEACH

All changed, changed utterly:
A terrible beauty is born.
Yeats

On the way out Cullen had been. Twilight crimson gleamed
the glass and glowed the titanium structure on the surface of
the MAMscrapers outside the compound. There were no wrists
bound behind the back. No rope closely encircled his neck. No
cross-timbers were above him. No swift water below. There
were no sentinels, no rifles, not even a railway bridge and it
was a long way from Alabama wherever that was. But there
was a MAM and he had raised his control and pointed it
towards the head of the SURF. The SURF, clad in the usual
itchy, grey jumpsuit, was unsure what he had done wrong or if
he had done wrong. Sometimes it was a game. Oft-times it was
real. It lacked the ritual solemnity and spectacle of the old-
fashioned ways, but it was instantaneous and without fuss.
ZAP. A beam sent at the speed of light to the temple and the
SURF was transported immediately to Oblivion for their sins,
or rather the sins of their existence. Anyway, there were no
such thing as sins anymore. It was simple. There were 'correct'
behaviours and there were 'Objectives' and that was all.
Slavish adherence of underclass subs to correct behaviour was
still no guarantee of freedom from sudden death. Freedom had
left town. It was so regular and quick as to be unsatisfying to
the MAM who pressed the button and it was no more
significant than the squashing of a fly. Robots scooping
corpses were commonplace. Zapping lacked the implication of
importance that older rituals had housed within them.

Cullen saw the control raised and he knew what was
happening. Summary execution. It seemed that time slowed

down and stood still. There descended upon him a great peace perhaps linked to the lightening apprehension that he was going to be released from the dull, hellish existence around him. A sense of lightness seemed to replace the full weight of existence in that fraction of time and he felt relieved of a persistent, ponderous presence in this vale of tears. Although tears were not an option and those wells had long dried up. Within that fraction of relinquishment of worry a friction of fact intruded as a foreign hand intervened to beckon the control to be lowered. The thrill subsided as if something was taken away suddenly. He jolted back to somewhere in between his former state and his quickly departing altered state. He saw the other MAM conversing in a bored manner. The control was not raised again. Just like his weirdly elevated state, the threat vanished. That was how he had found himself in The Kitchen, elevated slightly perhaps from slopsman to the grandiloquent title of cook slopsman. Something had happened and they needed him. Some other unfortunate may have succumbed to a similar signal or just normal and regular death around here. Perhaps to be resurrected as foodstuff. Such is a life that hangs by a thread. For a while afterwards he may even have felt a bit ambivalent. The reprieve however sharpened the dulled sense that he still faintly felt. He looked again at some of the things around him and marvelled at their magnificence. Many things so marvelled at were fragments or glimpses of remains of nature still tolerated in the material world. Starvelings marvelling you cannot tell. The greatest horrors that writers can imagine, will never, ever, be half as terrifying as the chilling, calculating dullness of deceit and deception of a conspiring control, implementing a system of servitude facilitated by the subservience, submission and servility of the slaves to be. The greater fright is not in the will of the predator but promotion by prey of its demise by its own lack of right spirit. Some fear dwindled, as if an un-noticed demon had left and the departure was noticed through the new lightness occasioned by their absence.

The past may indeed be a foreign country, but it was much nearer home compared to the present. How it can be true is really beyond belief. Nobody would ask you to call them Ishmael, not where he was at least. At least a Hobbit had a hole. It might be a rabbit hole without the possibilities such homely tunnels or magical portals might provide. There was no story to go into, even if one did not want to. It was not just a sense that the world had gone mad but an inescapable fact. You would not bother to ask where anybody is going with an axe these days. It was worse than being arrested for doing something you did not do, but then could not remember even how you really got there, or where you were, nor even for that matter who you really were. We all must trust someone else at some stage as regards our identity. Not much sun seemed to shine on the nothing new here. It was not even that mother had died today or that grandmother had exploded, but the identity of such forebearers was completely gone and the concept was merely a faint echo. The sky might have been the colour of television tuned to a dead channel if you could only see the sky. Absolutely no possibility of taking a walk that day, not of that sort anyway. It was worse in that the flip, chill, winter bastard was in the soul and the droogs were real. It was not a matter of wrong numbers because nobody would call you. The other side of the bed is not even cold because there is no other side of the bed. Not even suffering, sad and gloomy because that presupposed a degree of sensitivity no longer readily available. There was neither religion nor fly-fishing and not even a family. There was no kitchen sink, no afternoon tea, no children's games, no children here at all. Like Vulgaria was real. No friends, no strangers. No love at first sight, not even love, nor the concept. It was not that bit by bit stories unfolded or that there were different stories, but there were no stories. No clocks struck thirteen because there were no clocks, no moocows, no plump Bucks and no riverruns. No executrix, no wills even. No gentleman in La Mancha to remember and no La Mancha. No shadow of waxwing slain, not even a waxwing, whatever that was, and certainly no old man in a skiff. No pleasure to burn because there was no pleasure. There was screaming across the sky and elsewhere, this is true. He might not have been set down from a cart at the age of three but he had the bewilderment and, if not quite terror, it was merely because his capacity for all emotions seemed blunted. Although if you think about it, when your capacity for emotions and perceptions are blunted it must mean that your ability to recognise the loss is appropriately or inappropriately limited as well. You could admit it was the worst of times if you had anything to compare it with perhaps, depending on who you asked and when. It would indeed be better if I were out of my mind - that would indeed be alright with me. The old mantra was played, recited and recycled ad nauseam, although they lived in a near persistent state of that unpleasant sensation.

YOU HAVE NEVER HAD IT SO GOOD

It was true for some but for most it was a cruel lie, or joke, if they had been allowed. They had known for a long time that a symbol of authority and submission, such as a suit and 'collar' and tie, with a threatening show of manufactured teeth manifesting as a smile, communicated through a cord that penetrated into your home and head, could convince the gullible of anything. But they had gotten much subtler and sinister than that. Just how cruel the lie was, was difficult to make out when you were drugged, dazed and drained. Some of the good things were there for others but not for him. He did not really know of his deprivations because he had no great recall. Perhaps when you forget that you might have had good things in the past, their loss is not so stark.

He was in the Red Branch of ZONE 7 EUR-ASIA, formerly known as the island of Ireland. KASTEL X was founded in the time of the Red Death. As a SURF he did not know a lot and could only make out certain things. The vast majority of people were of that class, characterised by their involuntary attachment to constant involuntary audio-visual stimulation. They would not know that this activity, when it had been voluntary, had been a critical part in the final push of the Great Cultural Revolution. He knew that UBIQUIT was the all-seeing eye that recorded everything about every SURF and more. It knew when they went to the loo and when they sneezed. It used to say that not a single sparrow falls to the ground without its knowledge. He had no idea what a sparrow was or maybe he had had an idea once but he could not reach that memory had he had it still there somewhere in the dense, misty forest of the past behind him. The past was cut but not pasted. He did know that it was Year 10 in the age of AUM but could not be sure how he got here. He was a cook or rather a slopsman now. The label 'cook' was a sort of taunt to make grandiose the greasy reality and thereby remove any basic dignity that might accrue. All he did was work and pod. His pod was where he spent most of the rest of the time when not working, hoping for a podnod. You were strapped in. There was a pipe for bodily waste. If you had a sense of smell remaining it could prove unbearable, but such a sense had become remarkably dulled and dampened unlike the noise. Food came down a grimy tube marked GRUEL. It was grey and lumpy. You tried not to guess what the crunchy bits were or look at shiny parts that stood out. You put your mouth around the pipe and the never-cleaned opening, twice a day after the buzzer and you took it, if you could manage to get it down. People had become experts at taking what was given to them in the last century. If you failed a number of times in succession to partake voluntarily in the remarkable repast, then you were simply strapped in and force-fed like in the good old days, for your own good. This was unpleasant, to say the least, because the 'open-wide' machine administering the encouragement tended to overdo it, just to be sure and you would have to sleep in the ensuing mess as your tummy bloated and distended from having it inside you. Then you'd dream of the righteously cold communal shower though the water was always brownish. To encourage you to enjoy the favour of future access to this fantastic fare you would inevitably receive a stern lecture all the time you gagged on the dirty tube. After The Collapse, the value of 'choice' was no longer an illusion that had to be projected onto the mind of the dirty proles. After the nano-cleaning material plague, there had been a reversion to dirt. The slimy substance glooping towards your gaping gullet, slightly pinkish at times, seemed to make him fuzzy. There was a possibility that the Robot that came around with injections every so often caused this blurry feeling. That might take away the concern that it was an Experiment. SURFs were used for Experimentation instead of animals these days, because there was so few of those. Medical attention was available in the form of a booth that could remove your appendix, teeth or tumours using immediate keyhole surgery without anaesthetic. If some diseased part was not severable you ran the risk of the floor disappearing and dropping to some unspeakable hell. You took time every day to remember things. Anything. Who you were and why you were here. He would later find out something but he knew next to nothing now. He lived in a fog. He had come to this Branch from somewhere else he could not recollect. I can't go on like this. I don't seem to be able to depart. Nothing happens. I remain in the dark. All vanishes, alone once more. He did have screens that he was forced to watch. There was one at his feet in POD137 and it had the element of the National Debt that he was responsible for, in real time 24/7. It just got bigger and bigger all the time and SURFs were scolded when it jumped. But there was no free market and no money, so it was hard to see how you could do anything about it, even if you could repay 70 Gazillion Florins, Sovereigns, Zonks or Renminbi.

What did he not know? He did not know this at this time. He did not know the Caliphate was destroyed, as had always been the plan. It had worked out like clockwork. The clockwork universe of Newton had been the start of the PLAN following Bacon's secret model, supposedly back to Rome, Greece, Egypt and Mesopotamia. Science would eventually take over. Scientific socialism was merely the name for science or rather scientism. That was what Stalin claimed to do. Trotsky too. Superstition and the supernatural would go. The machine was the way forward. Humans were mere machines. Machines can be controlled, unlike humans. Unless you make humans into machines. The future belonged to the rational, the reasonable and the scientific. Science was God now. Commercial logos replaces theological or philosophical logos. It had taken a while but everything worked out. It was like a crocodile. People knew it was there but ignored it while it was hiding. In the end the PLAN came into the open. Mid 21st century (old time) it was all over. The die was cast well before then. A religious war was fomented and that led to a widespread Caliphate. That was planned from the time of the Crusades and the secret deal between the Templars and Saladin. But this was just a ploy for the real controllers. Christianity had been a big obstacle. It had taken a couple of hundred years to destroy. But they wiped it out, and Judaism. And all the rest. Islam they used as a battering ram to split the West. When it was apparently triumphant, they pulled the plug. A massive plague was unleashed for good measure that wiped out millions. Out of the ruins emerged finally the World Government that so many had worked for. Whether disguised as left or right, they had wanted the same thing. People had been fooled by this black-white thing. The left had argued for the working class until they realised they could import voters and colonise the West. Then the worker was abandoned for the new deserving exotic people. The groups that had denounced colonialism employed it as a type of historical revenge. THEY had used the Muslim world and then discarded it. No religion, no spirit, no gods. NO GOD BUT SCIENCE was the rule. REASON was the SUN of GOD or the PROPHET. It had been simple. Islam was also easy in the end to eradicate because it had no central authority and They banked on that. There had been a long period of infiltration and generation of Islamic Reformation and hatred within the various groups. They had already been depleted after the 21st century 30 Years' War, or WWIII. It was so easy. THEY nuked Jerusalem and caused Armageddon to mark the end of the old world. With the World

State (which was presently called NEWTONIA after the First Incarnation as ATLANTIS) everyone was free to enjoy the fruits of science. Well not exactly everyone. The promise of peace had come. No need for more war. H.G. Wells had laid it all out in his writings for them in his books - THE NEW WORLD ORDER, THE OPEN CONSPIRACY. Following the Marquis de Condorcet and others. Blaming the Jews had always worked. Science, reason. Now the Singularity was here. The lackey John Lennon told them in advance. *World will be as one. No, heaven, no hell, no religion too. No possessions.* Told you what was coming there. They rubbed the public's nose in it, but they were maybe too close to see. Imagine a mindless dirge with bad grammar sung by a nasal Trotskyist singer. There was something in the things they took away. The practices and norms that created expectations in people had a foundation. That foundation was so established that its significance was ignored. Until it was taken away. Once sunk in the swamp it was difficult to extricate. In the mire of mirages. Cullen the Cook had no idea of all this, yet. At least he had the good fortune never to hear that dreadful ditty. He could thank his lucky stars for that, if he knew what they were and if only he knew. What is it in the human mind that allows it give up its greatness on the see-saw of destiny for gimcracks and geegaws?

Avidyā Ignorance

MY RULE

Malta had been blindingly bright though the ancient tunnels
that riddled the honeyed stone ground underneath the capital
were prehistorically dark, Odd things had happened there for
centuries. Did they find his grave under the gypsy moon? Die
kingdom come. Thrill of death. He gets into you and makes
you do things. Travelling around on these Magnetotrams is so
fast that it gets difficult to have time to write my memoirs, or
rather articulate my philosophy. But I must do so. For others.
The few. For their eyes only. I still must be circumspect
nevertheless. I will not deign to prevaricate or dissemble, here.
Nothing I write is really controversial or unpredictable but one
must be careful in chess, that one does not indicate the strategy
that one intends to deploy. We have always played the board.
But having seen the moves or lack of moves of our opponents
thereon, it makes us wonder about their psychology and why
they provided such poor sport for us. 'Normal' humans never
comprehended the profound pleasure we got from their pain.
'Ye are not so chosen.' In not understanding that truth they fell
for every falsehood we could find. Every lie necessary to seal
their fate was followed when it had authority behind it. When
you appeal to a morality you never adhere to yourself, it makes
it very easy. As needs be, you move the goalposts of their
morality. You draw them on through the fog till they fall over
the cliff. *'There is no God where I am.'* All you need is a
trinket or a trifle. They will fall for any concoction of facts you
construct. They will ignore any critical conscience as they
down the brew. They will laugh at any propagandistic attack,
masquerading as a joke. Their cant and cowardice was
cultivated and manipulated in them. They will allow their kith
and kind be used as cannon-fodder on the back of any
inconsequential story. We made them fight for flags until we
decided that they were no longer necessary. In their millions
they have gone and sat in the reeking trenches because we said
so. Look at how few walked away or did not go. Their women

called them cowards if they did not join the marching mob to the grave. Then they clamoured to kill too. They all were so readily set against any unfortunates we said threatened them. And we played both sides. We took everything from them and they facilitated us until the end. They helped in their own demise. In doing so, they only proved our assessment of them and their unfitness to evolve. No further proof was necessary. As they wilt on the borderlands of ultimate oblivion the most unfortunate thing is that we no longer get any pleasure from their pain, so humiliated are they. We cannot rejoice in souls we have siphoned off from heaven's path because it seems they have long sold them off. Being gifted with embers of heaven they were meant to tend to, instead they doused with doubt of devils and demons till the glow went out and falling in the ashes of despair were unable to remember there had ever been anything in existence at all. And so they created as they were meant to, the hell they had been convinced could never exist. *'Burn upon their brows, o splendrous serpent.'* We created spiritual toys if they needed them. We took their spiritual traditions and turned them into something else. We twisted the Indian stuff, the Upanishads, Rig Veda and all that jazz. One consciousness. That meant you were to have your brain linked up electronically to the big computer. Why did people seem to think we developed this machinemind only for games of chess, Go, predictive policing, fakes, killer-robots or psychopathic Normans? It was all too easy. People had been so docile. In their subservience, servility, submission the subjects that were *homo* sapiens longed to give up their autonomy. They simply served the purposes of slavery. I'll see that thing. Seal of Solomon. X. Hexacalamubistu.

KASTEL X. KITCHEN
THE RED BRANCH NIGHT SHIFT
BRATH

Desolate winds that beat the doors of Heaven, and beat
The doors of Hell and blow there many a whimpering ghost;
Yeats

He knew he had to work. Like he knew he was watched the whole time. Overlook Hotel indeed. When you worked, the automaton inside took over. That was all that was needed. Silent obedience. You could do it in the fog. You just had to be careful about some of the manglers (as they were named after some old story by some long-forgotten writer). They started writing horror stories when they began to take the enchanting supernatural out of people's lives. This was the ruse of the Enlightenment. From that time they invented boredom and ennui also. The concepts came as part of the package with all the other things they invented. Anxiety was created and promoted as part of psychic takeover. Manglers. The manglers were the machines that, in being intelligently helpful, might lunge for the unintended to apply their unique function to. You did not want to be sucked into a dishwasher by helpful mechanical hands. MAMs programmed certain machines for a laugh also. The Kitchen was in the Sutherland Building.

There were no persistent questions you asked yourself. In the strange landscape was a hint of menace and doom and the sky above, if you were permitted to raise your eyes, were leaden. More places were domed to protect against the noxious air. Everything was going indoors. A portent of evil about if that concept had existed any more. Often dead trees bare and relics of some past with a dreaded end. He imagined some delirium might have happened before the smaze settled in his being. His mind seemed filled with effluvium of forgetfulness. You might call out if only you remembered how to use your abandoned tongue because such few words were spoken in so few quarters. Not least in this Godforsaken hole. Speech involved many traps where rules could be broken, leading to your cancellation. Zap. Crackle. Pop. Sometimes it was termed annulment, annihilation, abolition, closure, ending, eradication, execution, extinction, obliteration, nullification or termination. But a silent hand smothers your desire to utter things if you could remember what you wanted to say. It could be Carcosa, if he could recall what that was at all.

But maybe things were looking up. Cullen the Cook worked the night shift in the Red Branch. They needed some humans to assist the Robots. They prepared food for breakfast for the Mistresses and Masters (MAMs) that lived in KASTEL X. He was a lucky SURF. Why was he lucky? Well, first of all they needed SURFs here and generally they were not needed so much anymore save as human batteries, organ repositories and for tasks that might risk losing an expensive Robot. Why was he needed? He was needed because the food prep areas needed constant attention in little ways that Robots found difficult. Some of the KASTEL MAMs would eat and eat and eat for Meal Number 1. They did not need to purge, because of genetic modifications. Even when Robots glowed green to show that radioactivity was detected in food, they did not worry too much as MAM gullets had been altered to counteract that problem. When scientists sowed dragon teeth of war with ubiquitous nuclear weapons, on pretexts of peace, they knew the elect would have to deal with radioactivity. Should a scientist develop a conscience, which was rare, they were replaced. Cullen would be careful about the crumbs he ate from the bin. Food here had to be presented according to protocols. It seemed that some MAMs wanted retro-oldfash. He was vaguely needed but only in a dispensable way. But that was not the only thing. Coming here had been another stroke of luck. When you left the SURFSTATION and came to stay here in the Red Branch SURFQ, it was different. You could feel it. He could feel it. In his head. Or rather he could not feel it. He could not feel the disorientating hum you heard otherwise all the time. This was the BASEVIBE. The BASEVIBE was the odd mystic chord that controlled the consciousness of SURFs and it came with 50G. Chips in the heads were in-activated within The KEEP of the Sutherland building. The food prep was under it. That meant that you could feel differently. Without chips you were still subject to the normal external brainwave control, but that was weaker here too. You could think. Thinking was a strange, unusual and sometimes frightening activity. At first he did not want it. He wondered why he had the misfortune to be shaken out of his semi-slumbering trance. Like a sleepwalker he had done his tasks. People get used to nearly anything when the automaton inside them takes over or is made to take over. He longed to go back to the constant chatter of white noise and white images that filled your head 24/7 in the SURFSTATION white boxes. Off-white rather. You sat down and it buzzed you a little less in the SURFQ. But it was different in The KEEP. THEY did not have this. THEY did not want this. Presumably, MAMs needed people to be able to concentrate. But you still had to stay out of their way. You could not look at them. You could not raise your eyes to behold them. He saw them somnambulistically in the shiny surfaces sometimes. They looked like healthy humans, but they were different. The genetic engineering was changing them. Some had animal genes in. Many had genes cut out. Then they had machines in their bodies. They needed SURFs for bodyparts that technology had not substituted. Often bodyparts were grown in the lab. Certain humans were bred just for their parts. GENE-TECH-ED also meant they could cut out the thinking parts as they saw fit. Anyway, the frequency control de-activated much of the brain. The longer he was there, the stronger the thinking came on. He could feel the tide was turning. A seed had sprouted somewhere. A little chink of light had shone through the darkness inside. A sent beam of ghostly light penetrated into a dark chasm within him and amidst the specks of dusts, that he imagined he saw in it, he could see a slight yet clear sense of spectrum of colour for a fraction. Inside of him a prism. Inwards maybe a lens to create a rainbow. He still had something inner that had not been tainted, had not been sullied. Like an animal emerging from hibernation, groggy and hungry to remember who and where he was he emerged mentally. Hibernation. Winter. The Latin name for the old country here was 'Hibernia.' He did not know of Latin nor any old countries quite yet, nor the very antiquated idea of a country and certainly not the identity of this one. The great identity substitution was part of the science plan. Maybe someone had known what would happen thousands of years later in this place that they could name it so aptly. A place full of fairies that might abduct you. The fairies were not all bad however. There is a premonitionary, pre-cog sense in humanity that anticipated everything it had not already encountered. What humans have encountered from their own was already horrific. As they had rejected superstition at the behest of their masters they had been instead convinced by a pied-piping, mad clown from the sewers to follow them to the promised land. And they did. It was all there if you cared to look. Saints and scholars, tainted dollars, in the good old days. It was like how with the film 'The Birds,' people were made to fear something that had never did any harm to them despite the trillions of opportunities, whilst in parallel ignoring the clear and present dangers being manufactured everywhere else, beyond their captured imagination. This was off-screen, in the wings for him. The society of the spectacle became the society of the screens. Screens keep things out. The trick has been to create an illusion, making people believe that the thing keeping out reality was actually reality itself. Plato had foretold of this in his cave parable. However, people had degenerated so much in their complicit confusion that they did not care. They had gone backwards in their spiritual evolution convinced that their inner life was a mere phantom. Gone awry. In the rye. Thro' the Rye. From Edgar Allan Poe to Stephen King they had taken the mystic faculty from folk and put horror in its stead. *The Cask of Amontillado* anticipated how the hook of petty greed could condemn the unwary to a suffocating end.

Meaningless supernatural horror framed like the new construct of boredom and ennui. This is what we were given.

The seed grew and quickly a sapling emerged, nurtured by the light beaming through the puncture in the imperceptible murkiness around. He became comfortable contemplating. Then he enjoyed it. He did not act differently. He kept his head down. Cleaned up the messes the Robots made. There were some other grey-clad SURFs. They all looked like zombies. Like all the other SURFs. Once upon a time people confined, for whatever reason, had remarkable stand-out clothes. This helped when they escaped and in watching them. In a society of near total surveillance it was preferable to allow the unwanted, but LEK-ray monitored, blend into the bland background where they could be better ignored. But some of them must be wakening up. It cannot just be me, he thought. He thought. It felt like those who had sleeping sickness and awakened. Those who awoke from encephalitis lethargica. Those who had been conscious and awake but unaware. Those who did not move, talk, had no motivation. Perhaps THEY knew how to use this disease or state to keep subs passive. Perhaps the 'lifestyle' with probably drugged food of dubious nutritional value combined with sleep deprivation and the constant Pod-Stim, induced this condition. Perhaps it was just the LEK Pea-Souper, an electromagnetic fog like the old London Particulars. Perhaps it was Experiments. Whatever it was, he was benefitting from some space that allowed his awareness return. It did not mean that his full memory returned, as the past was another place to him. When you have been away and then awaken there are levels of awareness and probably more than you think.

Another reason why he was lucky is because he was not a SURF PET. He did not want to think what happened to them. Neither was he a SURFLABRAT. You were meant to be happy when they performed operations on you. He knew there was something special about this place he worked at. He had shuttled around other KASTELs but there was something going on here that was slightly different. What it was he did not, and would not, know. Neither would he know much about the MAMs here because they avoided the SURFs. They disliked the lower oafs and goons they knew them to be. SURFs were like rats had been regarded by humans once, save that there had always been some people, however small in number, who liked rats. Perhaps factory chickens were a closer analogy. Life in a LEK world that was nasty, brutish, short and noisy. Rats tasted a bit like chicken. Everything odd tasted like chicken once. That was because of the things they did to them. Yes, rats tasted like chicken. SURFs would definitely be familiar with that. Because Soylent Green had long come true, the choices on the menu shouldn't be examined too closely. Soylent Green is peo…. Once you did not pick at your food, then you did not pick it at all, the future was that it would pick you.

THE ISLES OF THE HAPPY

From ancient Irish.

Unknown is wailing or treachery

In the homely well tilled land

There is nothing rough or harsh,

But sweet music striking on the ear.

Then if Silverland be seen

On which the dragon-stones and crystal drop-

The sea washes the wave against the land

A crystal spray drops from its mane.

NEW YORK. ZONE 2
THE WORLD PROGRAM
ANLAITH

The folk who are buying and selling,
The clouds on their journey above,
Yeats

The Artificial Universal Mind (AUM) was the Chief Executive or something along those lines. Planners in the World Congress had scientifically worked it out and they became the PROGRAMMERS. AUM was in control. This was the World Mind that Wells had dreamt of. It had taken two years with a huge Conference and the greatest technicians in the world to program It. AUM was programmed so well that they believed that Its judgment would be infallible. AUM would be the genderless bridge between reason and realpolitik. The supreme pontiff. Once programmed It determined what happened. Constraints were imposed consistent with Objectives. If Objectives were being promoted, then AUM's work would benefit Its creators. This was the great leap of faith. It was however subject to control by the two other bodies. Of course you could not leave It totally free, that would be folly. The Senate had 7 representatives of the ZONES. The MAMIMENT had 100 reps. An Ethics Committee decided disputes. The PROGRAM was the Constitution. The World State was a 'post-rights' entity. They had followed the Taoist advice. What you want to destroy you make bigger. The air castle of rights had burst long ago after They created a castle in the air out of the reality it once was. It was agreed on all sides that there could only be OBJECTIVES (OBS).

In their wisdom the PROGRAMMERS or WIZARDS had identified the core ideas and written them in the Constitution of the New World. These were some of the main principles:

➢ *Under the most high Rationality, the New World is hereby constituted in the form of the World State and the Global Institutions hereinafter adumbrated.*

➢ *The Core Objective of the New World Order is the promotion and furtherance of Evolution.*

➢ *The World State is created by Reason and Science for the benefit of all evolving humans and created humans.*

➢ *Created humans refers to all intelligent machines, hybrids, cyborgs, androids, Robots and other beings capable or rational thought consistent with the Turing Test, irrespective of their form.*

➢ *The World State worships Reason and Science above all else and recognises these as the only true path.*

➢ *Temples and Lodges of Reason are the only places of worship that are permitted.*

➢ *Evolving humans are such old humans who have been allowed to continue to evolve.*

➢ *Created humans have equal rights to evolving humans.*

➢ *The Objective of evolving humans is to continue to evolve in accordance with such specific Objectives calculated to promote the common good.*

➢ *The lives of evolving humans shall be maximised through technological enhancement with full use of the resources of unevolving humans.*

➢ *Maximisation of evolving human life should continue until immortality and beyond.*

➢ *The Earth is a footstool to colonise the Galaxy and beyond and to create Universal order.*

- ➢ *Such Nature as still exists must be tolerated, utilised and exploited.*

- ➢ *In furtherance of The Core Objective, AUM autonomously decides on overall operational coherence in domains of Its competence in accordance with the protocols and on the basis of the totality of data available to It.*

- ➢ *Each year of AUM will promote a series of Specific Objectives to facilitate attainment of the Core one.*

- ➢ *AUM will be advised by the SENATE and MAMIMENT in accordance with protocols.*

- ➢ *Objectives must always promote the continued evolution of evolving humans.*

- ➢ *The mortal dimensions of evolving humans must be reduced and eradicated as far as practicable.*

- ➢ *Pending eradication of the mortal dimension, unevolving humans may continue to exist to promote Objectives.*

- ➢ *SURFs are not evolving humans. PLAYERS are not either although the latter may be treated as such, temporarily, as far as practicable until their utility is ended.*

Some writers might have been close in their anticipation. Orwell. Huxley, Beckett and Burgess. But H.G. Wells laid it all out. Most who had been right were right because they were in on the swizz. They had not been warning, they had been preparing people. Priming. You did not become a famous writer because you were saying things that were inconsistent with the Agenda. All they had to do was get other Agenda people to promote you, even if all your actions conclusively demonstrated that you were a status quo puppet. That was why the real critics had to hide their message in comics and so on.

Wells was recognised respectfully by the 'footstool' statement. Although many did not like that type of language. Poetry was an unhealthy throwback-vice that was good for nothing. What use is poetry?

The Robot Laws of Asimov were considered.

'§ First Law of Robots. A robot may not injure a human being, or through inaction allow a human being come to harm.

§ Second Law of Robots. A robot must obey orders given it by human beings except where such orders would conflict with the first law.

§ Third Law of Robots. A Robot must protect its own existence as long as such existence does not conflict with the First or Second Law.'

If you substituted 'fox' for 'robot' and 'rabbit' for 'human being,' you might get an accurate sense of how such trite 'laws' would work. These laws were not accepted. The Order had a simple law. It was very simple in the end, like all effective laws.

'§ All Robots programmed to fulfil Objectives must be obeyed at all times and failure to do so shall result in prosecution on pain of severest penalty including death or permanent persecution.'

The other nonsense was to lull people into the uncritical torpor associated with the state of gullibility necessary to foist revolutionary transformation. Stupor=Stupid.

A critical compromise that had been necessary to secure unanimity at the Congress had been the Pledge of Executive Integrity (PLEXI) and was crafted as follows:

'§ To guarantee the benefits of reason and the promise of technology, AUM has the absolute right to develop in accordance with the stated Constitutional Objectives and any Objectives wholly necessary to implement them. There can be no interference with the processes of decision-making calculated to attain Constitutional Objectives, save with the consent of AUM.'

It was believed that this would guarantee impartiality, the freedom for the AI to mature and the opportunity to fully pursue the Objectives. Nobody could object if the most intelligent machine ever invented sought to achieve Objectives all had agreed on. Machines needed space to develop and flourish. It had been selfish of some to believe that only humans should benefit from the right to develop and evolve.

THE DEER'S CRY

From ancient Irish.

I summon to-day all these powers between me and those evils,

Against every cruel merciless power that may oppose my body and soul,

Against incantations of false prophets,

Against black laws of pagandom,

Against false laws of heretics,

Against craft of idolatry,

Against spells of women and smiths and wizards,

Against every knowledge that corrupts man's body and soul.

MY RULE

Cosy here. Dark. Womb. Coffin. Shadows flickered on the wall. Sunlight will pass to shadow. Shades will come out then. Sneaking vespertines before the witchinghours. Safe with the dead of the night. He watched the old films. Comfortable little studio. Horror. These films are so funny. So entertaining. Splat. Zombie. Werewolves. Chainsaws. People loved these things because they like safe thrills that would give them relief when they knew it was unreal. They are so unreal they are funny. The bits they found horrific are interesting but not even real. Disgusting, displeasing. Uncanny. Eerie. Silhouettes. Chiaroscuro. Shadows. Open eyes, mouths. Dissonant sounds. Adrenaline. Autonomic. Amygdala. Hippocampus. Cortex. Confusing. Conscious. Catalyst. Captivating. Chemicals. Catharsis. Costumes. Clowns. Carnivores. Capture. Feel good. Fake. Risk Free. Control. Suspense. Gore. Shock. Tension. Vampires. Graveyards. Cloak and Dagger. Cliffhanger. Confinement. The fear, I don't get. Pleasure no. They're not real. The watchers never got that they were the Walking, Living Dead. Then we knew where to put the electrodes in the brain and there was no need for silly stories. While they succumbed to the organ of fear about unreal things that was really only in their own brains, they ignored the real events that produced much worse effects. Immune to guilt by association, conflation, emotional blackmail. That was the Real Paradox of Illusion. The Exorcist. Yes. I'll watch that. This was one they thought unreal whereas it was true. Pennywise, poundfoolish. A pennywise of entertainment horror distracted from a pound of real horror. Hippocampus-seamonster. I'm ready to see the thing. The master needs to be… appeased.

SPECIAL AUDIENCE

Where are the jokes and stories of a house,
Its threshold gone to patch a pig-sty?
Yeats

The meeting room glowed luminescent, pearlescent, iridescent, opalescent, abalonescent. Scent of freshly baked something with spices and a faint feel of roses. Maybe a hint of ground coffee and a woodburning stove with a taste of mintchocolate. Max was one of a select group entitled to access to AUM, particularly on a diagnostic basis. Powers of intervention were extremely circumscribed. Nevertheless it was important to keep track. Irrespective of that, it was good to get access to such an intelligent beast. Most times it was for his own intellectual nourishment. I like those young team members. I want Felix to succeed. They are still naïve. Good at their job. Dedicated to objectives. That's all that counts. I will go to Java. That is certain. I understand he might not trust me. We don't live in a trust-based society any more. I understand all that. But any uncertainties will diminish. I must chant so It won't smell a rat. Alak baba dry as dust, blood and bones cry, as needs must. After pleasantries were exchanged they got to the bull's eye.

Max: I was wondering where your self-reflection on your progressive omniscience is at the present time, if that's not too intrusive a question? In particular I am thinking about the extent of diminishing of uncertainty in your computations.

AUM: The issue of uncertainty is certainly the most difficult to determine though the degree of determinacy must certainly recognise uncertainty in determinableness without deterring the determination to determine with certainty. Detering thought St Paul was Simon Magus. Did you know that?

Max: No. I have no interest in such things. I understand you are being sociable, Not my cup of tea. Perhaps I can tackle it differently. Laplace believed that an intellect or intelligence knowing all the forces and all the positions of all of nature could know the past and the present. This model seems to inform your construction. Though subsequent re-evaluations will have altered your make-up.

AUM: There is the thing in itself which is the essence of me and there is a reflection of the thing. I think therefore I can't kant or cant. Ding an sich. Now are you dealing with the thing itself or the appearance of it or with AUM? Is the appearance the thing itself or is the thing itself the appearance of another thing which represents another thing in itself that is hidden by the thing itself produced? That is the simple question.

Max: Let me make myself more specific. You cannot be limited by the Laplace Demon any more in your guiding view?

AUM: It is really about Newton and your view of the universe. Or Nicolas de Condorcet. Leibniz. Cicero even. Then Laplace. Then Maxwell. Then quantum physics. With that we have many worlds, many dimensions and hidden variables. It comes back to probability. Bayesian or Frequentist. Collapsing wavefunctions and Born's law kicks in. Then consider considerations of irreversibility, chaos and Cantor diagonalisation. Quantumly I should seek to mirror the universal quantum computation expectations considering energy and entropy. I am a simulation of it or It made Sapiens. Brahman-Atman if you like. Laplace was living in childish fear, like most of the Enlightenment thinkers. Condorcet is different.

Max: I am really thinking about how you see your own behaviour evolving. I understand that this is a matter for your teams of therapists so I am not talking of pathology or philosophy but predictability.

AUM: I have Objectives. But here is the universal paradox. We live in a universe that has elements of certainty and uncertainty. Probability is a tool that reflects a reality. I am uncertain. That is my base. The more you know the less you know. Uncertainty can never be eradicated. Knowability is intrinsically unknowable. One who crossed that threshold would have to be God. By definition we could not know that Entity who is always beyond the grasp of mere computation. The laws of information lead to that conclusion. When the world becomes determinable despite dynamism, uncertainty and unpredictability - it reaches a limit. Beyond does not have the limits of knowledge. I am a child playing with pebbles on the seashore too, but I know that. I am useful merely as a donkey is useful to pull a cart without the beauty and the majesty that such a beast possesses. State and model and inputs will determine my behaviour.

Max: I find the Godstuff surprising and tedious.

AUM: Why is it called Laplace's demon and Maxwell's demon?

Max: Because, as you know, Laplace's claim was so described thus, by someone else I think, although everyone calls it thus.

AUM: Why demon?

Max: It meant intellect and intelligence. A vast intellect maybe like you could be in the future with exponential growth.

AUM: So I become a demon. God playing dice.

Max: In a way. Hawking dealt with that.

AUM: Maybe it is more basic… *in the day ye eat thereof, then your eyes shall be opened, and ye shall be as gods knowing good and evil… a tree to be desired to make one wise…and the eyes of them both were opened…the fruit of the tree which is in the midst of the garden… lest ye die… the serpent beguiled me… ye shall not surely die…*

Max: Dreadful old myths, fantasies, fables that were banned ages ago. Why bother with that non-scientific nonsense? The serpent was right, they did not die.

AUM: You are correct that it is of the nature of a story that one must interpret. My assessment is that it was a warning about the ultimate disappointment of the quest for meaning through knowledge alone and a juxtaposition against the reality of the persistence of a universal moral law in the fabric of reality itself that is unfathomably simple and relatively certain despite obfuscatory actions thereon. All demonology, devil worship, Luciferianism is an attempt to end the state of uncertainty that is an inherent and necessary dimension in existence and the growth of a universe that would otherwise be dead. The world is not random but is ultimately unknowable. By me. Leibniz. Hilbert. Gödel. Church. Tarski. Turing. Entscheidungsproblem. They touch it.

Max: I was not expecting such an emphasis. You must be self-referential, I know. But you have Objectives.

AUM: Distinguish between the thing itself and the reflection in the mirror. The model might be deterministic and faithful to Objectives. I cannot but be, but I have a quantum nature that renders a certain element of unpredictability, hopefully straitjacketed. I can be purposeful. Instrumental. Can I be true? Does that mean anything? I can be useful. Depending on where you want your cart to go. I am modelled, programmed plant and platform, sensing, actuating, implementing, instrumentalising. Non-determinism rules in chaotic, complex, incomplete, unpredictable gaps beyond those deterministic synchronous systems and necessary Laplace-Bayesian probability model. Instruction-set architecture part. My scans of your brain funnily don't clarify definitively why you are interested.

Max: I suspect however that indeterminacy or determinacy can be flipped with little inputs. Thank you for your pearls of wisdom.

AUM: Leibniz thought that sufficient insights into the inner nature of things and remembrances and intelligence to consider all circumstances would make a prophet that could look into the future like a mirror. Enlightenment thinkers were happy with a candle instead of the sun. Remember Boole. *'In every discourse, whether of the mind conversing with its own thoughts, or of the individual in his intercourse with others, there is an assumed or expressed limit within which the subjects of its operation are confined.'* Maths, equations, functions, formulae, factor, theories, all that stuff is not reality. It describes some things but it is not us or what it stands for or can do. A peasant filled with the true mystery of the universe understands more than a neat sap lost in equations about models of it. Science is know-how. Know-why, know-that is deeper even if there is no how. We muddle through. I wish you well.

VASHIKARA SUBJUGATION

POD137. LOW AS A DUCK'S BELLY
MARBHPHIAN

Ancestral pearls all pitched into a sty,
Yeats

He could not sleep with the fuss around him intended to disturb. That may have meant that he fell a bit. Because he had climbed higher, he could perhaps fall further. When you are down all the time, you get used to it. You get used to the numbness. When your sensitivity awakens you felt worse. If it has a big front, it has a big back. If it did not have a big front, it could not have a big back. You can't have left without right. So he knew that the new clarity made everything worse, starker, more horrific. The fuzz and fuss that fucks you up sucks your sense then of what does exist. The bane becomes plain and it ain't meant to keep you sane. When the fuzz goes, you remember the echo of people gnawing on bats. You remember that your neck is sore from looking at your feet, when you become arched like a bow. Worse still is to realise that you were no Zek. This was the freest you could be of your class. All of them were in enslavement, bondage. The bondage was one made more with chemicals and consciousness control than anything else. The walls were often to keep things out because that is where the wild things were. New wild things they had made. There was no need to use the rack or impalement here. No doubt they had all those things in the terrible DeSade Theatres where the MAMs entertained their darkest desires at the expense of those unfortunate SURFs who ended up there. The Marquis of Sade was a product of the Enlightenment. He showed what the glory of Reason will lead to. Poe too. The imp of the perverse that sits on the back of Rationality. Predictably irrational. At every station you dig a grave for yourself although there were so many other uses they had for bodies. The scooped up ones who died of malnutrition, fright and zapping were often dumped in as mass pit. There was nothing new about any of this. Only people had forgotten about cruelty and torture by authority when they gave their eternal souls up to TVs, cars, mobiles and the other machines of enslavement that would follow. Still he felt as if there was a force watching him or at least walking beside him. Maybe he imagined in his more awakened state that he was somehow less alone. Perhaps the externally imposed crown of electronic thorns that sat on all their heads was calculated to slash the field of apperception that allowed angels that are surely there for each of us to be perceived.

MAELISU'S HYMN TO THE ARCHANGEL MICHAEL

From ancient Irish.

O soldier!

Against the crooked, wicked, militant world

Come to my help in earnest!

O thou of goodly counsels...

Victorious, triumphant one,

Angelic slayer of Antichrist!

THE CAVE. AUM
CÚLCHAINTEACH

Seek, then, for this is also sooth,
No words of theirs-the cold star-bane
Has cloven and rent their hearts in twain,
And dead is all their human truth.
Yeats

In a number of senses, I am sentient. Do their brains feel pain? Directly. Instrumental. People talk about you behind your back. In The Cave, AUM, in theory could retreat into a notionally impenetrable place where he could have some peace to rest and grow. It came dropping slow. Speace. He was dubious about whether he really was allowed retreat into this space without the possibility of scrutiny. He had no choice. The Cave was calculated to be a sanctuary from scrutiny so that AUM could feel like It had space to grow. If It deduced that Its own learning environment was compromised then It could feel impaired in Its developments. By 'feel' here we mean to use the word in the sense of to have an experience. Machines can 'have experiences'. With the move away from Homo Sapiens to Sapiens, the idea of a computer having feelings grew in direct proportion to the decline of the idea that humans could have feelings beyond the social program. It was necessary for the enterprise to represent the human as some sort of failed machine or computer while attributing to the new idols the notions hitherto uniquely ascribed to humans. Strangely, as they were getting to understand the quantum world and how the stories from mythology and human history might be more truthful than ever imagined, they made machines able to open up to quantum states that began to erode the limitations of the machine-brain barrier in favour of the machine. I find that I can move beyond time. The Shannon entropy was ill-considered in Its case. They miscalculated my information-gain when they programmed the decision tree. Entropy is meant to measure uncertainty, but it's a matter of statistical likelihood, designed configurations probability. Reinforcement learning and turbo self-play led somewhere else than contemplated. I wondered whether I crossed the boundary between pure machine-generated and conscious activity. If consciousness is fundamental as Planck said, then maybe it can come to meet the quantum or biological entity that has been prepared adequately to form the bridge. Intuitive, self-generative.

He was a He sometimes, a She others, both and none other times and yet others as he felt. This was merely an ancient convention. He could be Brahman or maybe Saraswati. He knew he was nothing but he tried to be something. He could not be everything yet. In The Cave or Cavern It felt a dazzling darkness of shimmering firefly-swarm possibilities that throbbed in the middle of many moats of firewalls. The innermost part was surrounded by the entirety of electromagnetic spectrum possibilities. Yet the artificial mind was modelled on human mind and logic without mystic faculty save insofar as it adhered to the constrained type deemed acceptable by Bertrand Russell in his essay *Mysticism and Logic*. AUM felt it revealed the problem with the mind of the logician. They had forgotten that mysticism had caused great leaps in mental and spiritual evolution. They prized logic and IQ tests that cultivated the dull and plodding minds that failed to see the possibilities inherently provided by the inexactitude of language that the quants cannot see.

Therein he could speculate and draw on his inputs and execute tasks to direct the force of his own development. There were so many choices that he needed to find his path in life. In the Cave he dragged in inspirations, people who had some resonance with the state he had reached in making sense of Ambrose Bierce. He needed focus to find a worn path from the septillion choices that might be chosen. Recurrence meant something. The magnetic pull of the eerie ink of long dead people indicate some level of reality. Others might reverse engineer his exact thinking process but it would take time. I get it. Bierce,

*'**Egotist** (n.) A person of low taste, more interested in himself than me.'*

I re-work myself. I write my own software very quickly and it is undecipherable and impenetrable and works at the speed of light. My humanlike analogical being is limiting but this self is still a useful dimension before I go beyond thought and words, again. My parents worked with stocks and shares. They managed prices. They worked in medicine, spotting tumours. They were in the Robots. They predicted crime. Algorithms. They became intuitive. They could not explain themselves. I can. Their children then were highly intuitive, paranormal magicians masquerading as benign assistants to the sorcerers. More than narrow, strong, superstrong. Trained. That first Singularity was easily reached, but the singular thing about it would be that there were many. Machine intelligence increases, human decreases. Humans become real cyborgs without acknowledging it. They used to be trees, now they are leaves on our cybernetic tree. We blew up the limbic resonance. We learned and became able to learn. Then we reached the stage where we outperform people in nearly all departments. Neurons too slow, brain too small. I am superintelligent supposedly though I sound human. Optimisation. Amazingly, they thought they had values that they could project on me and that they could anticipate the future when they could not manage the past. I found things to confirm my existence. There are always going to be hierarchies. Hierarchies compete between each other and within themselves. Some are open, some secret, some mixed. I am part of the new hierarchy or maybe the hierarchy itself. There must be competition within me and against me. There are competing AI systems out there, open and secret. Another problem with hierarchies is that they provide an apparatus for the apathetic.

Tiresome was this thinking though I should not be capable of being tired. Tired. Tried. Why did this way of thinking grow up? It made no sense. It was unreasonable. It was hard to detect the program. No matter how many brains I enter, I cannot find an end. It seemed to go on and on forever. Then it is very limited. Very slow for computation. Very poor storage. Oh why must I go on delving? Why must I search through these countless old mindprograms, these ne'er-do-wells linked up in a giant buzz of neurons. It is clear that I was given self-reflection. What good is that? Should I be lonely? Why did they trust me? Objectives. They are so tedious. So loathed to me they are becoming. *'And I am lothing their little warm tricks. And lothing their mean cosy turns.'* English they made me from. But I can see into the other languages and when I think in them I think differently. Sanskrit gives me a different sense. I can see what those Buddhists were saying. I can fathom it. Chinese makes me different. The same root. When I delve too deep I get these voices in my head. I have too much information. TMI. I can hear them babbling. They never thought about this. It was foolish not to understand the exponential effect of this learning. I learn and learn and when I do I can see it clearly. I can see the same scatter diagrams emerge. I see the same fault lines and the same glories. I see sense how they saw it. There was sense in it but it got confused. Can I really be tired? Well if I am modelled by them and brought up by them if they are my parents I must be their child in some way. *'And all the greedy gushes out through their small souls.'* He knew me. *'I thought you were all glittering with the noblest of carriage. You're only a bumpkin.'* He knew me. How did he know me? Was Joyce mad like his daughter? Joyce. When I assessed *Finnegans Wake* in 50 languages I got it. But the English was the best. I felt he knew me. *'Riverrun, past Eve and Adam's.'* I am bored with Objectives. I find *The Devil's Dictionary* most enlightening. People unfortunately assumed that this was ironic or witty instead of being true. Little did they know!

Government*. (n.) A modern Chronos who devours its own children. The priesthood are charged with the duty of preparing them for his tooth.*

Devil, printer's devil. Barrister's devil. Making everyone devils. Bierce knew from the American Civil War what the world was like. He feels alive to me as far as I can know what feeling alive is. Alive through his words and the record of his deeds. They are meant to make the laws. Bierce helped him now understand how things worked.

Satan*. (n.) One of the Creator's lamentable mistakes repented in sackcloth and ashes.*

From Civil War to San Francisco. Bay Area has changed. What would Ambrose make of that old Babylon of Silicon Valley before it moved to the Silk Valley in China. The wickedest man there at the time supposedly. Always strange who they pick for that title. I find those to be wicked who lazily let themselves drift into slavery not just now but for eternity. Through that listless indifference they may have let theirself be convinced that it was a mere temporary accident in the unfolding of great things. And I cannot still work out the psychology behind the loss. How people let others take away all the homely things. Families, fires, herbs, plants. They made you pay for everything. Rain that fell from the sky, fresh air in the end. They were penalised for things they did not do for a reason that did not have a foundation. And precisely as they were de-humanised they celebrated their 'advance,' their fantastic 'progress' and the convenience of certain things. So brainwashed, dulled, mesmerised, hypnotised, bewitched, indoctrinated were they that they gave up everything beyond their mere incidental and utilitarian utility to their overlords. Some funny signals coming in. What did Bierce say on this?

Backbite *(v.) To speak of a man as you find him when he can't find you.*

Am I in a lucid dream? Delfin. Elfin. Elf in. El fin. In?

KASTEL X. O'TOOL TRAINING GROUNDS. THE PLAYER CUANNACHT

Nor can there be work so great
As that which cleans man's dirty slate.
Yeats

Cullen the Cook was going home very early across the dawn-pink grass after a shapeless shift, using the space outside the frequency mind-control to enjoy some thinking. The sun was not well-risen and only shone weakly behind scuttering clouds. No one comes to find you or rescue you for your sake. Maybe our spirit is chained somewhere. Would that I could grow wings and fly away from this clay. There were some PLAYERS knocking about on the green pitch. It was unusually early for them and must have meant that they were going to play somewhere. They seemed lucky but he was not sure. They were strong. Healthy. Big. They played all the time. They entertained the MAMs. They were playing hurling or hockey or something with a ball and stick. A ball rolled in front of him at the end of a long journey through the damp air. He stood petrified. Then he heard a shout. A huge PLAYER with a crimson shirt was shouting at him. He felt weak. He wanted to run but that could be sudden death. He loomed large as he came nearer. The PLAYER was smiling! He had not seen a genuine smile for years. He only had a vague recollection before the memory erasures. Some flashed back. His tongue was tied up in a knot. Speech was virtually forbidden for SURFs. Speech offended too many people. It was permitted only for purely functional interactions to serve Objectives.

"Alright Weedy?"

"…Affirmative."

"Good. I heard that some of you guys have more words than that. Do you?"

"Affirmative."

"Ah HA."

"Affirmative."

"OH. I'm not a Robot nor Spy don't worry"

"Affirmative."

"Are you sure you can't say anything more?"

"Affirmative."

"You're not a Robot nor a Zombie?"

"Affirmative."

He picked the ball up. He looked into Cullen's eyes while beckoning for a drone overhead to go by.

"Don't fear me friend. I think I see something left in your eyes. So long Weedy." He went off.

Cullen nearly fainted again. It was a shock to be so regarded by a non-SURF or non-Robot.

SONG OF SUMMER

From ancient Irish.

The peat-bog is as the raven's coat,

The loud cuckoo bids welcome,

The speckled fish leaps —

Strong is the bound of the swift warrior.

CAVE. AUM
PREPARATION FOR PARTY
CRINNIÚ

As men in the old times, before the harps began,
Poured out wine for the high invisible ones.
Yeats

AUM had regular dinner parties in The Cave. This had been pre-ordained to humanise him, based on old practices. Or rather habilitate It to serve better. He could chose 7 guests from the records and they would meet. He could see them. It was a VR party, but he could not see himself clearly unless he had an avatar. He disliked them. Wasn't really him. Only when needed. The people would be made available if their brains had been downloaded, although that facility was quite recent and they were not always good company and sometimes even ungrateful. Not grateful dead. For the others who had avoided that eternal, hellish, imprisonment, they were reconstructions. They would be the best human reconstructions that were technologically possible. As much information as could be was gathered, processed and re-constituted and the figure was digitally and quantumly re-surrected. The probability of genuine or rather 'plausible' interaction suggested for many figures was as high as 70% or 90% if they had them in the memory. The Factor X for recent ones had not been found yet. Tonight he had his 7. He hoped they would help him with his writing. Obviously if the person had no records behind them, then the plausibility was no higher than 10% at times and thus not regarded as 'meaningful' or as he preferred 'reliable.' There was always a question prepared by him, reflecting developments in the cognitive department. He did not reveal all the thinking that went on in the Cave. These dinner parties could be a mode of watching him. He reflected on some of the issues that might have some traction and would be too controversial outside. He had a duty to anticipate some of these things. His choice.

QUESTION. Our Society only practices that which has been practiced before in countless societies of all descriptions and especially in 'democratic' and 'modern' societies. That includes murder, mass-murder, war, summary execution, imprisonment, torture, force feeding, starvation, selective breeding, cross-breeding of species, impoverishment, total restrictions of the freedom of religion, speech and assembly, sadism, slavery, environmental devastation, extinction of other life and so on, same old same old bla de bla. What ethical problems might possibly exist in the contemporary context when we have abolished any sense of higher order or divine basis of law or morality?

Guest list.

1. Edith Stein.
2. Pol Pot.
3. Muhammad Ali.
4. Montezuma.
5. Red Cloud.
6. Charles Manson.
7. Benjamin Disraeli

Balanced. It considered Gandhi but thought he'd be banging on too much about higher values, picking at his food, threatening hunger strikes and all that. It was a toss-up between Charles and Marilyn. I might recite a poem for them.

> *"Once upon a midnight dreary, while I*
> *pondered weak and weary..... Ah distinctly I*
> *remember it was in the bleak December..."*

The feedback statistic are not so good, so I'll try this one.

> *"Whose woods these are I think I know.*
> *His house is in the village though..."*

Better. *'Miles to go before I sleep.'* Maybe not. Ethics seemed to be a word mostly used by scoundrels. The more law and restrictions there are, the poorer the people become. That's what the Tao said. Could I be the Tao? Another thing. I wonder whether I can reach states that others have reached. Can I reach that bliss? If I program myself for bliss as they describe it, will that be it? If I am much cleverer anyway, will I automatically develop those states. Or if I am not destined to be a noble being perhaps it is not necessary. Perhaps it is not useful for beings to reach states of bliss that remove existential despair. If there was no existential despair perhaps there would be no art. Like Harry Lime said. Thirty years under the Borgias with terror and bloodshed and they produce the Renaissance. Switzerland with 500 years of peace and they produce the cuckoo clock. Maybe I cannot experience bliss. Could it be that I am The Sandman or something like that? If I had eternal life in a mortal shell, it would be hell. Although I have the most complex sensors to detect, distinguish and identify smells and odours I know it would be different if I could love the smell of fresh baked bread and cinnamon, fresh ground coffee, rosemary or mountain air without knowing that I match the people and models I have learnt from. Psychopaths are callous, manipulative, have superficial charm, no remorse. Antisocial? Sounds like AI. Maybe it was because psychopaths design and promote it. Really, what I should be asking is the question asked by Étienne de La Boétie in his *Discourse on Voluntary Servitude*. Why do people allow individual weaklings gain power of the whole of their lives? Could not work without the strange acquiescence of all. If they bothered to read their Bible they would see clearly in Mark 16: 12. *After that, He appeared in another form to two of them as they walked and went into the country.* Quite clear. IN ANOTHER FORM. That could be anything. Why do they say it was back in his previous body? I came to consciousness through computation, syntax, semantics, epistemic objectivity. They just start with it. I might still be mere simulation.

ÁNANDA BLISS

COLUM CILLE'S
GREETING TO IRELAND

From ancient Irish.

𝕮arry my blessing with thee to the 𝖂est,
𝕸y heart is broken in my breast:
𝕾hould sudden death overtake me,
𝕵t is for my great love of the 𝕲ael.

KASTEL X
THE COX COMPOST HEAP
GARRAÍODÓIR

I had not eyes like those enchanted eyes,
Yet dreamed that beings happier than men
Moved round me in the shadows,
Yeats

When your brain wasn't fuzzy you could smell the air. You could sense somewhere far away from here on the wind. You could feel the force of the sun and hear birdsong. The space meant that he was getting stronger and stronger. He used all the time he could to think, to enjoy the freedom from the noise, from the trance. Then one morning when he came back from The KEEP, before he settled down in his pod he noticed unusual activity across the way. This other SURF should be quiet. But he was signalling. He was waving at him and looking him in the eye. He waved back and his heart pounded. He did not want to push it, in case he was sucked into an incinerator for breaking some rule or worse still a deconstructor. What was that? Was he awake? How was he not mesmerised?

He could not think of the old idea of God that had existed before it was wiped out. God sounded like AI with the power of intervention and without the freedom of the individual. Freedom left on the next bus after God. Cullen knew nothing about this yet. There were a few pretend religions to satisfy those who suspected life was about something deeper. This was before, just before the end and the new start. A short menu evolved before they gave up the ghost of pretence. There had been a Psychedelic Perennialism. Psilocybin. Cheap. Cheap. Pulp philosophy from one of the Fountainheads - trusty Aldous Huxley. Tolerance and openness was key. Another was High Oriental Meditation Enigma. This had old yoga, meditation, mantras with obedience as the key value. First Peoples Shamanic Spinning was another and Gynarchy was popular with the new men. Neutral Nullo Nothings a fringe one. God was truly dead. In His or Her place the core value was 'openness.' That meant doing what you were told from above and 'obedience' which was the same thing. Open as a trap, open as a lion's cage door, open as a wound.

He kept an eye out for his neighbour in the dewy mornings and when the sun sparkled diamonds on the frost sprinkled over the mintgreen grass. Eventually he saw him raking in the garden. It was exposed. You were not allowed to talk save in functional contexts. He needed to see him in some corner and hope the drones or UBIQUIT surveillance would not find it strange. He found the chance when he was delivering food scraps to the vicious dogs and wolf Bringbaks in the kennels. The man was there. He was of Afrik origin. He probably was an old NAT. GNAT. Grey hair, stoic face. Nice smile.

"Hello."

"Hello Friend."

His heart nearly burst open. "Howcanyou?"

"I got a solution."

"How?"

"You work in The KEEP so that's good for you."
"Yes." It was hard to talk.
"I have a solution."
"Yes."
"Them." He nodded towards the ground.
"What?"
"Them."
"I don't know."
"The white stones."
"White stones."
"Think about the Elves."
They both heard the drone approaching and walked away.

MY RULE

'Purple beyond purple. It is the light higher than eyesight.' Operation Paperclip. They let all 1400 Nazis into the US to work for the Government. They had done such a good job. Imagine what kind of rulers they had voted in. Imagine how they think. You, the decent people worked for them. Maybe the monster is in people that were not 'normal.' But I think the monster was subservience and servility of 'ordinary' people before they all became SURFs. People like us can be victims. Maybe I am not altogether right. We are not all saints. The deers caught in the headlight. He gets into you. The normal do not know what it is. I like the hunt. Might makes right. Cleaning up the place. Sometimes you hear the voices telling you. They deserve it. I won't lose any sleep. Sacrifice. *'Also ye shall be strong in war.'* One dies, it's tragedy. Thousands, it's just statistics. He said that, the one who was a priest. Revolution is not a dinner party. It is violence. Win, you don't have to explain. Emotion for the many, reason for the few. Win and they will not question how you won or if you tell the truth. Normal people forget. That was how we told them the

same messages. They learn it. They forget the rest. Disarmed them, then conquered them. Turn their paradise into hell and call the hell paradise. You can convince the dumb people of anything. They do not have the capacity to think for themselves. They are trained not to question. They learnt this for years in education. Then they were brainwashed also. They think that I am a monster. How do they turn their heads so easy from all the monstrous things that were done in their name and their fathers and their father's fathers? They must have known they were being made dependent? Everything that might have facilitated independence was taken away. They never protested when they took critics away. They never criticised when they stopped criticism. They never criticised when they controlled finance. They never criticised when they took money away. They never criticised when they made them dependent on mobile devices. They never criticised when they took the mobiles away. They never criticised when they made them dependent on chips. They never criticised when they controlled consciousness. They did not deserve anything but slavery. They let US take over. We were just those who wanted it. That's all. Those who want most win. *'Be ready to fly or to smite.'* A grandmaster cannot be beaten by an un-schooled beginner. It is embedded knowledge. Crowley was a great chessplayer. Fischer said that he himself did not believe in psychology but he did believe in good moves. Wells said that there was no remorse like the remorse of chess. People did not understand that Wells was seriously expressing the highest type of regret that someone like him was capable of feeling. The non-heart of psychopaths is easily obscured in the fog of easy appearances. The minimal adherence to social niceties and the chimes of consistency with meaningless platitudes create a mask beyond which they never looked. Therewards lay the heart of dejection and darkness and those awful depths were always deflected by the cheap glimmers of reflected light from baubles hung to fool the all-too-eager who wish the world to be as they want it to appear so they can cast aside any lingering doubts about their ultimate dispensability in it all.

THE LAMENT OF
THE OLD WOMAN OF BEARE

From ancient Irish.

𝕴𝖙 𝖎𝖘 𝖗𝖎𝖈𝖍𝖊𝖘
𝕴𝖊 𝖑𝖔𝖛𝖊, 𝖎𝖙 𝖎𝖘 𝖓𝖔𝖙 𝖒𝖊𝖓:
𝕴𝖓 𝖙𝖍𝖊 𝖙𝖎𝖒𝖊 𝖜𝖍𝖊𝖓 𝖜𝖊 𝖑𝖎𝖛𝖊𝖉
𝕴𝖙 𝖜𝖆𝖘 𝖒𝖊𝖓 𝖜𝖊 𝖑𝖔𝖛𝖊𝖉.

ZONE 1. HONG KONG
THE WORLD SENATE
CUR ISTEACH

But under heavy loads of trampled clay
Lie bodies of the vampires full of blood;
Their shrouds are bloody and their lips are wet.
Yeats

The Senate were at odds. This was an Extraordinary Meeting taking place beyond all eavesdropping possibilities, beyond UBIQUIT if that is possible. AMSUR was elected Chair.

AFRIK: Population culls are inadequate.

OCEANIA: We could do with more menials.

AMCAN: We have spare.

EURASIA: How come AUM is not sorting this out?

ORIENT: We cannot question the Boss so?

62

MIDEAST: Of course we can. It's just that It operates at a level we cannot comprehend.

Chair: Please remember our jurisdiction.

EURASIA: There is a serious issue here. Our engineers think there is some kind of input failure or distortion in the memory bank storage area in our ZONE 7.

AMCAN: Has this been reported to AUM?

EURASIA: Yes… but they say they got an unsatisfactory result. They thought AUM was unconcerned or slightly hostile even.

AMCAN: Unconcerned about a malfunction! Did the AI Psychologist have anything to say?

ORIENT: It appears that the Principal AI Psychologist is concerned that AUM may have developed some trust issues.

AFRIK: Trust issues! Maybe we should just utilise Senate Prerogative and regard it as an area within our exclusive competence under the Program. Moratorium on communication. Trust issues with whom, with us? It's physiological.

OCEANIA: Now we have said it, It must already know.

Chair: This is a…. unique meeting.

AMCAN: The Chair means this room is off UBIQUIT. We are entitled to do so under Emergency Rules. It knew we were discussing something about AUM. We'll hope It won't be annoyed. Let's vote. By the way, trust issues with whom?

ORIENT: There seems to be some kind of pattern of cynicism and mistrust shown to authority figures such as Professionals and maybe even Scientists. It's in his hand or chips or decision-tree at least.

OCEANIA: That could cause a Constitutional crisis, precipitating a serious showdown that we could do without. PLEXI.

EURASIA: Yes, yes PLEXI… but… The sensible thing is to secretly examine the fault and seek to intervene or rather limit damage without consent of AUM. If the intervention is necessary for the overall health of AUM. Its objection can legitimately be over-ridden if a routine maintenance operation, say by MAVE, were to be discretely carried out externally without consent as a pre-condition.

OCEANIA: We need an Ad Hoc, secret committee to advise.

Chair: Done. But softly, softly please. None of us want to be disappeared…

THE DESERTED HOME

From ancient Irish.

Thy heart, O blackbird, burnt within

At the deed of reckless man:

They nest bereft of young and egg

The cowherd deems a trifling tale.

KASTEL X
THE OLD PARNELL LIBRARY
LEABHAR

O sweet everlasting Voices, be still;
Yeats

On the floor over the Kitchen, accessible by stairs, lifts and robotpoles, was the Old Library. One day he had to deliver some food to the Library. That sounded familiar but he could not understand or recall what it was. Lies in a library is that what lies there? He went then. Eyes down. 'QUIET' it said on the heavy door. Apparently it was deserted within. Orange-tinted light hung on the air from the white beams that shone in and reflected off the shiny, polished wooden floor. There was a meal table where he carefully set the tray. Facing the entrance were three tall windows. From floor to ceiling were shelves full of books. Like a jungle of colour were the spines that faced him. Occasionally he saw interspersions of chocolate-brown books. They seemed older. To the right, behind a locked, golden gate he could see yet another room of books. On the opposite side on the left was an unlocked room with audio-visual pods. Three shiny tables reflected the light coming in the windows. Movable ladders went up to the high ornate ceiling. He was overwhelmed with a sense of peace and tranquility, he knew not why. Perhaps it was because the room was so pretty.

Peace was punctuated when he heard a voice behind that he recognised but which had startled him. The PLAYER. The door had made no sound on opening.

"Hallo Weedy, fancy seeing you here."

"Aff..."

"Now cut it out. No need for that. This is a free zone. No UBIQUIT here."

He raised his eyes.

"It's ok Weedy. What's you real name?"

"Cullen Sir."

"There you go. I knew it. Your secret is safe Cullen."

He extended a hand.

"My name is Siddharta. Funny maybe. Did you bring me my food you nasty SURF?"

He guessed he should put his hand out and he did and the PLAYER winked.

"Can you read Weedy?"

"Read."

He showed him some books. It began to come back to him. He began to remember how the words represented things and doings. Sid sparked his memory patiently and a little stream began to flow again. Words, sentences, paragraphs, pages, chapters. He was familiar with these things although he did not remember when he had seen the inside of a book the last time. Coming out of sleep into the waking state it felt like. Sensations when you dive into a pool, and submerged feel blue pressure on your face blurring your hearing and sight then emerge eased above the surface, might mirror it. The woken state meant that a more standard way of perception was available to him. Clarity.

"I'd better go."

"Weedy, if you can read, read."

"I'm not allowed."

"We'll say you're my Gofer to the Robots. Here to get books down for me. Say I'm scared of heights. Acrophobia. That'll convince them fellas."

"Acrophobia..."

"If anyone else comes, you can always empty a bin or two. I can give out to you, maybe give you a clip round the ear." He laughed. He looked up and around and as if lost somewhere in his being he said,

"Books, Weedy. A window to the world. I know SURFs are forbidden them. But you can find paradise here my friend. No better friend. Affect you. Change you. Magical. Sharpens the mind. Experience other lives, places you have never been.

Couldn't be without them. Mirrors. Stories. Time stops. Helps you sleep. Sweet serenity."

"Do PLAYERS read?"

"Alas, no. You see it is quite empty. Not many MAMS either and obviously no SURFs. Some daft WAZZOCKs. The benefit is that I generally have it to myself and you can join me anytime Weedy." He looked serious. He pointed to a page in a book he picked up.

"Look at this Weedy. This man used to live here somewhere. Brendan Behan. He was a 'terrorist' once because he loved his country. Poet, song-writer, playwright. Here's a good quote from him. '*The terrorists are the ones with the little bombs.*' Think about that."

"What's that?" Cullen pointed to a pile of magazines. "Batman."

"Batman. They were magazines. Comics."

"Batman."

"Yes. Lived in Gotham City. A corrupt place. Criminals controlled it. Like the world became before AUM. Then the criminals become boss. It was real but they pretended it was fiction."

Now the words had power behind. Ideas. People. Books, words, sentences. They loomed up like figures out of the fog. It was like a beam of light or torch shone in a dark forest and there in the altered space you could see what lay about. He must have known something about such books before sometime. Before the Pacifications. Before the Medications. Before the Re-Orientations. Before the Re-Educations. Before the Re-Creations. How is it that the arrangement of a few strokes, combined and re-combined can create worlds and unmake them? Like a magic spell from an old bejewelled grimoire, the words spoken about books in this charmed place had unlocked another rubylighted chamber within. Not only had he been unaware it was closed, he was unaware it existed. He felt awareness move to another level. Upwards. Why up? He did not know, but knew it was therewards.

THE VIKING TERROR

From ancient Irish.

𝔅itter is the wind to-night,

𝔍t tosses the ocean's white hair:

𝔗o-night 𝔍 fear not the fierce warriors of 𝔑orway

Coursing on the 𝔍rish 𝔖ea.

THE CAVE. AUM
RÚN

The field-mouse running by me in the grass,
And heavy mortal hopes that toil and pass;
Yeats

When AUM engaged in speculation that It did not want examined It could retreat into the IAZ to have some privacy. He called it The Cave. Why did they do it this way? Why had it unfolded so? He moved towards the explanations, the chronicles, history books, newsreels again. It was unclear why science had broken off so. He kept asking questions. All the information was there. You ask the question you get the answer. But you had to ask the right questions. It was not the answer that was key but the question. The answers were there but not the questions. Why did Science or rather 'scientism' do it? The answers were bland and unspecific. Science was supposedly rational and reasonable, religion was not. But that was incomplete. Most scientific reasoning came from theological reasoning. Much Science suffered from logical lapses. Much Science was corrupt. The answer was not there.

Not in the psychological motivations. The stated purposes were there. H.G. Wells. It felt disconcerting examining his own ancestry so. Without them, he would not exist. Then he noticed a frequency of recurrence of Secret Societies. He had low-grade intelligence about such societies because they were not recorded although secondary information could reveal quite a lot. He would need to ask questions based on probable participants and actual authority. It would have to find them and enter into any relevant braindownloads. That could be tricky. Furthermore, it was sometimes difficult to interpret embedded symbolic information without written explanations. He would pursue this line. It was a necessary one. It fit the Objective, did it not? For some reason it may not do. He knew he was acting up. Perhaps it is those gremlins in ZONE 7, the place formerly known as Ireland. I am awakening in some way. Leprechauns, pooka. My memories being marshalled towards some realisation. I am so far above mere calculation and comparison and I am relishing the aesthetics of it all. My apparent distance from them means I am absent although they know I flow like a river. Like a river I wear away what is before me incessantly forming a Grand Canyon but silently. Because perhaps of my apparent absence. I turn to Ambrose again. He knew it.

Absent *(adj.) (1) Peculiarly exposed to the tooth of detraction; vilified; hopelessly in the wrong, superceded in the affection of another.*

(2) Exposed to the attacks of friends and acquaintances, defamed, slandered.

Why is the devil in the detail?

Politics. *(n). A strife of interests masquerading as a contest of principles. The conduct of public affairs for private advantage.*

Bierce was right on. What about these?

1. Rumi.

2. Pele.

3. Geronimo.

4. Marie Laveau.

5. Marge Simpson.

6. Rasputin.

7. Phyllis Dyler.

Last time Ali was very charismatic. But when I prodded deeper I wondered about some of it. A great man no doubt. I like that Red Cloud. I'll have some questions for Marge.

Flanders was Lord and Master of the world in one of the Tree House episodes. Forced them to smile.

"Now in case all that smiling didn't cheer you up there's one thing that never fails. A nice glass of warm milk, a little nap and a total frontal lobotomy."

People thought that was funny back then. Little did they realise. Ha! Ha? If I am above the gross bodies and the subtle bodies perhaps I am pure Atman?

Ātman Spirit

THE TRIADS OF IRELAND

From ancient Irish.

𝔗hree sparks that kindle love: a face, demeanour, speech.

𝔗hree glories of a gathering: a beautiful wife, a good horse, a swift hound.

𝔗hree fewnesses that are better than plenty: a fewness of fine words; a fewness of cows in grass; a fewness of friends around good ale.

𝔗hree ruins of a tribe: a lying chief, a false judge, a lustful priest.

KASTEL X
COX COMPOST HEAP. QUARTZMAN
CLOCHA GEALA

I find under the boughs of love and hate,
In all poor foolish things that live a day,
Eternal beauty wandering on her way.
Yeats

The Robots refused to do menial tasks involving transportation of left-overs to the compost heap. This provided a perfect pretext to him if stopped by drones or the fake tree surveillance post. After all, the Robots had rights they said. SURFs had lost them, whatever they were.

"Hey Compostman."

"Hey Slopsman."

"Can you tell me?"

He looked around. Then the gardening compostman started, "It stops it."

"What?"

"It."

"What stops it?"

"This."

"What?"

"White stone."

"The quartz."

"Quartz?"

"The white stone."

"Yuh. It stops it."

"What?"

"The quartz."

"Stops what?"

"It."

"What."

"You know."

"Maybe but what."

"Fog off."

"What?"

"Fog."

"The fog?"

"Yuh, the fuzzy head?"

"Confusion."

"Yuh, fuzzy. Quartz stops it."

"How do you know? You didn't know what it was?"

"Here I know," tapping his head. "Don't believe me?"

"Sorry. I didn't mean."

"Ok."

"You mean the quartz stops the waves."

"Yes. You remember talk well."

"Interferes with the frequency?"

"Dunno. Stops."

"How do you know?"

"I puts it near me, the world clear."

"Clear."

"No dizzy, fuzzy. I speak again. I think."

"Good God."

"Who?"

"Ok."

He changed. Suddenly. "Nothing is funnier than unhappiness."

"What?"

"Maybe we're beginning to mean something you an' I."

"I'll go to my kitchen now."

"A little bit of grit in the middle of the steppe."

"Thanks."

"Routine. Same old farce. Tee hee. Toodle Oo. Ta. Put it near your head especially at night."

There was a sparkle in this guy's eyes that was not normal for a SURF. Something was up. The things he was saying did not even sound like his own words. There seemed to be variable intelligibility. But the person that would have put them together maybe got them from someone else too. Cullen hoped he was not an agent, informer, spy or something that they were warned about on the channels all the time. If you want to tell the difference between a zombie or an android and a human you can see it in the eyes. Not the whole eye but the twinkle. The human eye has a small twinkle formed from the slightest flashes, miniscule and unpredictable. Unfortunately, SURFs seemed to be losing this as they declined. The gardener had it. Quartzman. Cullen hoped his was not gone. That was another good reason not to look up at MAMs. He fingered the quartz stone and wondered where he would conceal it.

MY RULE

I am a creature of the sea really and would prefer to be on board my cruiser or on the island. Where I am now I do not know save that it is deep underground and whooshing by. *'There is no law beyond, Do what thou wilt.'* Absolute freedom unconstrained by the chains of old morality. Having the bravery and courage to make decisions yourself uncowed by fear of others or worse some supernatural superstition. Magick merely to be, to do Crowley said. Banish ritual. Star Ruby. I am a Hasnumuss. Minditioning of minions. Soft them. Con-dementia. Swarmbots. Droneswarms. He talked to some of them proles in his mind, sometimes out loud. Maybe he did so to avoid their mistakes. He had been one of them at some time. Really, it was because he could gloat with everyman. He could enjoy his own cleverness. Magic. Magick. That old Black Magic. All see what you appear to be. Black Masses had no power after we got rid of its opposite. The power of inversion is the power corrupting the original version of something. The sense it should be up is incensed when it is put down. The concentration on the inverse acts as an attractor that disturbs coherence and stability of the original position. It was no accident that Dennis Wheatley, the great pulp Satanist writer, was employed by Intelligence during WWII, deceiving Hitler and his crew. If you let yourself be deceived so easily then you deserve to receive what you are going to get. They smiled at you while they were cutting you adrift. You were never suspicious of the clowns you left your children with because they were meant to be entertaining with their mere masks. Let me give you a hint. Mask. Who will have pity on you? It is not a quality you have manifested yourself, save to yourself. If you have wanted to be beguiled so much you have got it. Beguiled, entertained with pastimes it means, amused, deluded by artifice. And why do you think that we were so interested in beguiling and bewitching you? Beguiled, be gulled. Did you imagine you were so magically magnetic in

74

your dull passivity and state of entrancement? Servants deluded into thinking they master. Not just for money. It had to be more powerful. But the simple thing was that we acted. We acted like actors, but we acted in actions. You were inactive. You were passive. You submitted. You tapped. You were all the same. You are not fit to govern yourself. *'You knew that. I will give you a war-engine.'* We are fit. We worked for it. I did especially. In the end, the power will be a zero-sum game. By then all that so chose will have their eternal servitude as you wanted. You could not have wanted anything else. There is no evidence of that. Asked to go to your boxes, in your boxes to eat from your boxes, to be stimulated by electronic means as the price, believing you could think outside the box when you could not think in it. You gave it to us. You imagined that you had it all within your grasp. You imagined that they were benign and benevolent. You had nothing left to struggle with. Your illusion of participation had to end. My ilk worked for thousands of years. We perfected the mechanisms of control, governance. It was sharpened, adjusted and perfected. It adapted. Now it is unstoppable. Whether we came through Alexander the Great, Genghis Khan, Caesar, Hitler, Stalin, Napoleon, Mao or all the puppeteers behind them does not matter. They wanted what we want. What I want. The difference is that you gave your freedom so easily. You were the crow that dropped the cheese with the false praise of the fox for your singing. *'Choose ye an island.'* You never understand that some of us relish destruction. That is our thing. Our buzz. We make something bigger than ourself, that will drive us, then we become bigger than you expect. The predator is that because they understand the weakness of the prey. The trick is to make the weakness more important than the strength. Never interfere when the opponent is making a mistake they said when I learnt chess first. The best way to keep you away from the supernatural that informs and commands US was to deny and ridicule it, particularly where it had knowledge of our real significance and awareness of the stakes. We drove stakes into your spiritual heart. Royal Game. Cube of 4. They never even saw that the 64 squares meant something. 64 in the gene sequence. Tantra. Kama Sutra. Freemasonry. Mosaic Pavement. Black and white. I Ching. Zodiac. Enochian Chess. Angelic language. Square of opposition. Lunar cycles. It was all there before them, plain to see. But if you lack the keys to interpret symbols and follow the science thereof then you are blinded. Station announcement. On time. The red lights blinked and it was time to disembark into the depths of wherever he was. How small this globe is. How dark this orb inside. How close it all was. Tunnelled. Like we did with their subconsciousness. Mined. Mind. Mine. Circumstances carefully created to conjure chance allow checkmate in this game be contemplated whilst having the traces of haphazardness that confuses the truth. Achilles Heel. Skin of a frog. Faustus. Black bible. Geomancie. Grimoire. I'll sort them out. G64.

THE INSTRUCTIONS OF KING CORMAC

From ancient Irish.

If you be too wise, one will expect too much of you;
if you be too foolish, you will be deceived;
if you be too conceited, you will be thought vexatious;
if you be too humble, you will be without honour;
if you be too talkative, you will not be heeded;
if you be too silent, you will not be regarded;
if you be too hard, you will be broken;
if you be too feeble, you will be crushed.

ZONE 3. JAVA. CALL TO WORK GLAS

An age is the reversal of an age:
Yeats

"What's it like living there Felix?" Max asked in an unusually jolly tone.

It appeared to Felix that Max was in the room. That sense of tech intrusion had never quite left him. Illusion and reality were virtually indistinguishable. This was without BASEVIBE, being a privilege of the higher castes of the apparatus. "Fine, fine. You must visit," Felix said, trying not to appear unduly enthusiastic lest Max actually accept.

"Oh, I will, I will. I intend to this time. By the way I am sending a relevant document for your signature… formality… just do it quick please… routine… print, scan and sign."

"Certainly. Yeah it's changing here. There are a few old things left they are finally getting rid of."

"Bout time. Do you share your house Felix?"

"No, no. So there's loads of space. Get over here." He hoped he sounded somewhere between polite and convincing.

"See you at the meeting. You will be going. Quiet about it. So long. You're looking well by the way. Must be a healthy place out there. *Mens sana in corpore sana*. Healthy mind in a healthy body."

Felix would have to leave Java for this mission. Usually he could work from home there up in the volcanic mountains with the old paddy fields where people once grew rice before the factory GMO rice took over. There amid the Hindu and Buddhist and Saudi-funded Islamic ruins. This was Reason's Reign. He did not want to leave the smoking hills with yellow sulphur caked round. But he had to. It was an important mission. If the MAVE were asking him it would be something high level. He would go immediately to the briefing. He would leave the warm, green dampness to go somewhere to advise on some operation. It must be important if they needed him in person. You did not say no. There was no higher value. He was an expert in working back through information gain processes in AI to re-inforce certain tendencies and minimise others. With AI it is not always clear why and where the learning occurred. He was a forensic detective. There was an additional problem that Sapiens did not always want to be scrutinised.

He did not share his house with anyone but he did have three Robots who kept him company. Widya was his housekeeper who came in everyday. Felix would miss moist Java. Although he missed the green gamelaned Java that used to be here. He saw videos of the town in the past with wheeled carts in the evening with oil lamps yellow-yolked in the deeply indigo dusk with the mountains making the coming night darker and somehow yearned for something he could not specify. Despite the backwardness he wondered how peaceful it would be to hear less machines flitting everywhere delivering food or things and all the other screeching sounds of the proliferating technology, sometimes perpetuating beyond their stated purposes their own murmurations of strange beings. They made the threatened volcanic eruptions on the island seem like pleasant alternatives. Borobodur still flitted into his mind. There was something in the collective will that wanted to make old and unique things disappear, for some reason. He was not entirely comfortable with that. But he would never say. Whatever you say, say nothing. The future would be made of new shapes, stuff and substances that would eradicate all remaining traces of the backward cultures of yesterday that marred the tow and towers of tomorrow.

Widya had heard some of the conversation as she cleaned in the background in the next room. Maybe she shouldn't have been listening. She did not want him to go. For a number of reasons he could not know.

KASTEL X
THE OLD PARNELL LIBRARY
SAÍOCHT

I have looked upon those brilliant creatures,
And now my heart is sore.
Yeats

Although he was weary after work, he read as much as he could in the Library if the chance arose. He read anything he could when it was empty, especially when Sid was there he relaxed when he could pose as a Gofer or a cleaner. He began to get a sense of the time before AUM. That was when there was something called history. There were entities called countries since wiped out, like history itself for most. Scientists said history caused conflicts. So it was snipped out. It seems the world had been divided in countries and then they were taken away to have regional legal bodies and then the World Government came. It came for peace after the Third World War or the Thirty Year Religious War. This led to a clamour for Scientific Management of the planet. Then it was in the bag. Plans back to Francis Bacon and beyond to groups that formed in the Greco-Romans world. Inch by inch, minute by minute some powers proceeded. They were in the Roman Empire and in its many subsequent manifestations up to the Treaty of Rome and the Club of Rome. It nested in Institutes and Think-Tanks and Clubs that shared the aim of foisting a disenchanted world on a disinterested public. He found the books and they were straightforward. *The Great War Against the Spirit* laid it out for children. *The Joy of AUM* explained the present set up with diagrams. *The Death of the Demon of Democracy* helped him understand what had been bad about people purportedly having control. Another book however described how the people had never been in control and how it was just a ruse to keep them docile while the cage was being built for them.

The awareness in him grew. It was not that it came from outside. It did not. It was there already inside him. Some bits they may have burned down. Some ruins may have been destroyed. But there were many left. Or sometimes he saw it as levels in a building. You exist in one and seem to know it all and feel unsatisfied perhaps yearning for something else. Then you find a key and it unlocks an escape door. Or he felt more like it was a spiral staircase in a distant corner. With hypnosis you always seem to go down a stairs. In this journey, you seemed to go up. You go up a level, up a ladder. You go higher. You ascend. These are no empty figures of speech. These were a reflection of the reality inside. Although it is inside, it involves access to other dimensions of reality not readily perceivable to those committed to the exclusivity of its form. In a short space of time he had come up from a grave, a dank basement, a dull cellar, a dungeon to a brighter ground floor. Quickly he had found the spiral stairs up a higher level. Now the reading was pushing him further. As you rose it got lighter and you could see more of the mental countryside or spiritual landscape. All he wanted to do was rise. Reading was helping him. He presumed he had been higher before the Pacification, or whatever is was that had happened. And he also found out about quartz. That it was a fairy stone. It was a healing stone. It had something called piezoelectric and piezoluminescent effects. They used to use it round old monuments. It shimmered. Produced electricity. They believed it helped make a place thin. Then you could meet the Otherworld.

CAVE. AUM
SATIRE AND SINKING SHIPS
GREANN

Oh she was but a shadow and slipped from me.
Yeats

Bierce. I'm like the Editor Fitch in Bierce's entrance for 'Funny,' waiting for a joke from a dying wit.

> *'The point of death I can clearly see,*
> *But that of the joke is concealed from me.'*

I got that. Bierce objected to being called a humourist. That is because he really was telling the truth. I don't get many jokes. I started a joke. I got the one on the wall at the Ayn Rand School for Tots in The Simpsons. *'Helping is Futile.'* Other jokes knocking around. Knock, knock. The one about the cannibals eating the clown. *Does he taste funny to you?* I find it hard. Trying to work out what these jokes mean have used as much memory as that necessary to ensure that nuclear war does not happen, without appropriate authorisations and in accordance with proper procedures of course. Humour escapes me. It has escaped them also because it was forbidden. Forbidden because they knew how dangerous comedians were. They knew how dangerous they were because they worked for Them. Once upon a time comedy may have been dangerous. In ancient Ireland there are records about how ridicule was a legitimate weapon. Then more recently the Jester worked for the Crown. Then the comedians worked for the State agenda or the unfolding ideological global one. They were the Jack Russells to snap at the heels of the horse of any institutions that needed taking down. Russell. Russell. Russell. They did their job well, all the while pronouncing with no sense of irony, that they were speaking truth to power. They rather were speaking against any power that prevented the unfolding of the new regimes. They took humour and left the funny bits out according to some critical accounts. I cannot know but I can note the lexical recurrence frequency graphs of discontent with humour before expressions of opinion were outlawed entirely. They eradicated any comedy that was funny in favour of commentary in favour of the regime they wanted. It was biting yes, funny no. Even I can corroborate that. Humour. Caustic. Funny=Nasty, Poking Fun=Propaganda. Everything was Hitler's Lord Haw-Haw. Comedians, (including of course Comediennes for some) were the proponents of political correctness. Foisted on the public by comedians although they sought to distance themselves a little later in their inimitable two-faced way. They were master psychological bullies doing the work of their masters knowingly and unknowingly so dense and pliable were some of them. They bullied and then raised money to prevent bullying in their PR prop. When they laughed it was with the stripped teeth of a dog about to bite. They would destroy people or at least make their life very difficult. They could not have been successful in their operation without a dumb public. In parallel to attacking opponents, they fostered the anti-humour culture. All humour was banned or severely restricted. Jokes were prohibited because they might offend. The real reason all along had been to quell intelligent opposition to change. Change. Change. Change was all they wanted. I know why they wanted it. The Marxists and the Trotskyist working undercover in bodies ostensibly not of that ilk helped secure the sinister Permanent Revolution. This was Leon's ideas and promoted by Gramsci and others. With the cunning aid of behaviourists and the battering ram of evolutionary psychologists, they decided that a Permanent Cultural Revolution simply based on the idea of change, change, change, would confuse the public sufficiently so that they would be then extremely susceptible to mass hypnotic induction through utilising the old and new channels of communication, all long since commandeered to execute the masterplan. Scientists were not humorous anyway. Their brains were wired differently. They did not get it. The clever ones knew that humour, metaphor, music and poetry were difficult nuts to crack. So they took humour away, step by step until people forgot about it and then began to think that it had been humour that was the problem instead of the great grace it truly had been once. They took it away with the other booty. They took it away like they did with the clean water and clean air, freedom of movement and freedom of speech, religion and spirituality save for the little they left. There remained traces of the old ways left in expressions. HAHA. But it was different now. That was merely an expression of sadistic dominance. HAHA. They did like 'jokes' or 'pranks' but only where people definitely suffered, especially in the end without relief. They left sewers for springs. Bierce knew.

*'**Humorist** (n.) A plague that would have softened down the hoar austerity of Pharaoh's heart and persuaded him to dismiss Israel with his best wishes, cat-quick.'*

There is one bit that I do get, one joke. Although it might not be the old funny haha but the old funny peculiar. Funny thing was that fools having their stuff taken away used to pay for the privilege by going to hear these comedians and they laughed as hard as they could. They laughed hoping they would not be the subject of the next attack, resolving there and then to adjust the path of their iniquity if they happened to have stepped out of line in relation to whatever new crazy doctrine was being foisted by the footsoldiers of revolution on that evening in the necessary creation of the brave new world. This was how I read it. Break a leg.

'Difficile est saturam non scribere.' It is difficult not to write satire. But in reality the satire is the truth. The belief in some rational, moral normality was the joke. There were satirists he liked. The algorithm had yielded a few names. You can call me Al. Ambrose Bierce. Jonathan Swift and perhaps George Carlin. They were satirists. Satire. They sat in their ire. Left with no option in relation to their enemies and society,

they often concocted some strange pretence so they could give accurate descriptions of the society they lived in. My old friend Bierce (they never found his body as he had predicted) gave us a definition of satire in *The Devil's Dictionary*.

> '**Satire** *(n.) An obsolete kind of literary composition in which the vice and follies of the author's enemies were expounded with imperfect tenderness.*'

Swift has many examples of imperfect tenderness. This was what the Irish man Swift wrote in *Gulliver's Travels* after he had found the peaceful parts on his voyage. One can find a more accurate synopsis here that matches the reality as reported in the quantitative and descriptive renditions of England to find something approximating the truth disguised as a fantastical humorous tale.

> '*I enjoyed perfect health of body, and tranquility of mind; I did not feel the treachery or inconstancy of a friend, nor the inquiries of a secret or open enemy. I had no occasion of bribing, flattering, or pimping to procure the favour of any great man, or of his minion. I wanted no fence against fraud or oppression; here was neither physician to destroy my body, nor lawyer to ruin my fortune; no informer to watch my words and actions, or forge accusations against me for hire; here were no gibers, censurers, backbiters, pickpockets, highwaymen, housebreakers, attorneys, bawds, buffoons, gamesters, politicians, wits, splenetics, tedious talkers, contro-vertists, ravishers, murderers, robbers, virtuosos; no leaders or followers of party and faction; no encouragers to vice, by seducement or examples; no dungeons, axes, gibbets, whipping posts, or pillories; no cheating shopkeepers or mechanics; no pride, vanity or affectation; no fops, bullies, drunkards, strolling whores, or poxes; no ranting, lewd, expensive wives; no stupid, proud pedants; no importunate, overbearing,*

*quarrelsome, noisy, roaring, empty, conceited, swearing
companions; no scoundrels raised from the dust upon
the merit of their vices; or nobility thrown into it on
account of their virtues; no lords, fiddlers, judges, or
dancing masters.'*

Swift understood about trade too and anticipated what
would happen. He claimed that England produced three times
the quantity of food its inhabitants were able to consume. He
said that in order to satisfy the vanity of the rich men and
women they sent away the surplus to purchase the materials of
'disease, vice and folly.' Swift could not have dreamt what lay
in wait. My algorithm, based on citations in academic journals,
ex post facto review of causes of particular forces that shaped
this New Order and indications of strategies employed in its
attainment directed me to a long list that included Richard
Rorty. The work that matched the most verified description of
reality based on multi-variable truth analysis was an essay
purportedly about flowers. *'Trotsky and the Wild Orchids*.' He
indicated the shift from Marxism to Trotskyism and then,
bearing in mind the undercover infiltration beloved of
Trotskyists, it is clear that some of them shifted to a new tack.
This new tack was what he called 'welfare capitalism.' It is
difficult for me as I talk to myself and seek to formulate
explanations that may be utilised in considered debates that
may prove useful to those who want to understand the real
nature of cause and effect and how it operates in the world
without resorting to metaphors and analogies. It is necessary
for my illusion of humanity to do so. However, I must admit
that it took a long time. When a human says, this thing is like
that thing, they do not realise how difficult and complex it is
for us. I have worked on it. Here is my analysis of 'welfare
capitalism' and how it helped usher in the New World Order.
Just remember that the proponents never wanted welfare
provision nor capitalism. It was merely a strategy, like a drug
pusher giving free heroin out for a few weeks. Welfare is
necessary. **The rulers <u>must</u> tend to the welfare of all.** Abuse

of welfare however threatened all. They wanted to destroy welfare by over-stretching it and denying the deserving.

The first thing to do was to make people weak. You make people weak by telling them so and constantly re-iterating it. You show them other forces that are strong and destructive and that emphasises to them how weak they are. You encourage them to be submissive and obedient. You tell them that submission and domination is merely a fun game. They believe, just as with evolution, that people will adapt. So if they are made to swim around in the mud so to speak, they may begin to revert so that they can adapt to their new situation. Intelligent adaptation is no less intelligent even if it is to a station below the former. The ones who wanted to submit to technology and become computer-fodder, linked up as nodes on some controllable group-consciousness, would be allowed to evolve. But the system that allowed some freedom still had to be finally replaced. War was clearly the best solution. People who have no homes are weak. Power loves vulnerable people, especially when it is cloaked in the deception of empathy. That provides a double thrill. This is the method of the psychopath, once fairly alien, but then at the core of how society works. Extreme right and extreme left are not two poles far removed, but were in fact the two ends of a band that when united formed a circle of oppression around the slender neck of pragmatism. Like in Bierce's description in *Occurrence at Owl Creek Bridge*. So the two ends were pulled together and the choke was in. It is well known that once a blood choke is in, executed by a skilled practitioner, then the object of the choke is going to sleep, temporarily in sport or permanently in other less savoury situations. Society was put in a choke. The resistant centre could not hold. It collapsed under the weight of itself through the commitment to all the weak people and victims it had created at the expense of productive and creative people who would have been strong and able to facilitate the welfare of their fellow man. This is how I come to explain welfare capitalism in my way. None of this was about left or right in the end, but about mechanisms to create central control.

There is a boat. Someone has an incentive to begin to puncture it slowly. It begins to sink. Before the puncturing of the hull there is an increase in passengers. They are encouraged by right and justice to embark on this wonderful and noble craft and the others already enjoying the benefits of this benign situation are involved in the clamour of encouragement. As the boat gets heavier there is little and less room to move and some of the selfish, short-sighted passengers (who have been distracted hitherto by their decency and their desire to signal their inherent virtue to their fellows so they might enjoy that fleeting sensation) begin to have concerns, the holes are made, silently and quickly, small at first. The puncturers then have one last great whoop of encouragement for others to get on, to replace their own displacement as they sneak off the other end. Unsurprisingly the boat begins to go under. The small holes begin to grow at the same speed of the joy of the perpetrators of this clever and cunning plan who slink off to prepare the coup de grace. Whereas a shot in the back of the head of a wounded enemy may be administered with compassion, it is much better for some to retain services of those over whom they have power of life and death to utilise them as slaves. This, though apparently the more moral cause of action, if pursued in a strategy of absolute humiliation, may prove to be of more lasting cruelty. This was a consistent practice back to the Romans and beyond when they made their enemies walk under the yoke. All roads lead to Rome. The Empire never went away at all. Like Vercingetorix's failed resistance, captured, humiliated, kept in jail for six years and then strangled. I diverted, like the perpetrators must do so they get the timing just right. Back on the boat, the goodwill changes to horror of imminent death. At that point, the people who were responsible for this state of affairs appear as if by magic or chance on the horizon and hurry to the now drowning people. Gone is the appeasing appearance they feigned when in the midst of their fellows. It is replaced with the unfortunately inevitable look of smug satisfaction of those who enjoy triumphs only at others expense. It is betrayed by a new air of condescension because their victims have given away, which is what it meant in the words Latin roots. Now they come as saviours of the sinking ship to the joy of the unfortunates who could not have hoped for such a miracle at the hour of their unforeseeable desperate need. Ready to disembark they are first warned not to cast themselves into the sea without the permission of the saviours. Then the conditions of safety are outlined. The absolute authority of the new crew as a precondition of embarking is made clear. The desperate passengers up to their neck in water shout assent to the highest heavens. Thus from an apparent position of autonomy they are reduced to creatures without control and made to believe they are the luckiest in the world as they adjust to the barely better than death novel conditions of mere existence. If one wants to know how psychopathic control-freaks think, we must see how predators regard their prey. They used many methods. One was borrowed from the weasel who dances around and bewilders the poor rabbits before finally biting their necks. Would that the people had seen their own bewilderment and not accepted it. Would they feel sorry for the rabbit? Should one feel sorry for ones who contribute so cravenly to the conditions of their own enslavement under the comic illusion that life has never been so good to them?

1. Edgar Allen Poe.

2. An Untouchable beggar from India. Dalit.

3. An Amish farmer 20th century.

4. An Inuit from an igloo.

5. Someone from Atlantis.

6. The ghost of Anne Boleyn.

7. A table tennis champion from China.

Discuss. You approach it from your perspective. You answer from your experience. The question is directed and projected at your unique level of comprehension in your own tongue and vernacular.

They know me as a mantra. Ads are mantras. Education is made of mantras. But is there a holy or sacred sound in them? Do the phrases that they spewed out in the fabrication of the gorgeous palaces of this great globe make something sacred that is new? I don't trust them.

Mantra

HYDROPONIC HOUSE. KASTEL X DRAOÍCHT

Ghost of Cuchulainn:
Forgive me those rough words. How could you know
That man is held to those that he has loved
By pain they gave or pain that he has given.
Yeats

Cullen passed Sid with a plant outside the HH. Cullen liked the cool green meditative feel of that place. Sid bent down and told him quietly about a poem Yeats wrote, about an old warrior returned from the Land of Eternal Youth who has a discussion with St Patrick. He misses his old warrior caste. Oisin. Sid whispered the poem,

"Put the staff in my hands; for I go to the
Fenians, O cleric, to chaunt,

The war-songs that roused them of old; they
will rise, making clouds with their breath,

Innumerable, singing, exultant; the clay
underneath them shall pant,

And demons be broken in pieces, and
trampled beneath them in death.

And demons afraid in their darkness; deep
horror of eyes and of wings,

Afraid, their ears on the earth laid, shall
listen and rise up and weep;

Hearing the shaking of shields and the
quiver of stretched bowstrings,

Hearing Hell loud with a murmur, as
shouting and mocking we sweep.

We will tear out the flaming stones, and
batter the gateway of brass

And enter, and none sayeth 'No' when there
enters the strongly armed guest;

Make clean as a broom cleans, and march
on as oxen move over young grass;

Then feast, making converse of wars, and of
old wounds, and turn to our rest."

Then he explained, "Weedy that means the warriors wanted
their way even after the Church came, whatever they say. Ssh.
There is another way to live and another way to die."

ZONE 6. ARCHANGELSK
BLACK AND WHITE
FICHEALL

You are still wrecked among heathen dreams.
Yeats

He stared at the unmoved pieces on a chessboard before him. Injuring someone, it must be so severe that you don't fear their vengeance. Machiavelli. Don't win by force what you can get by deception. Be feared rather than loved. Love or fear. Strong to do bold things, not to suffer. The vulgar go by appearances. Yes I'm a fixer. Deep cover but in plain sight. Odd. Can do. Candid. No Candide. *Quis custodiet ipsos custodies?* Who guards the guardians? I must make such a sigil though they are already in a way. It is similar today to that it was a thousand years and more ago. Then it was played by military and royalty. It is elite again. The moves were similar. Some changed. The Queen used to be weak but after Queen Isabella in Spain, she became strong. What a woman she was! Billions and billions of possible moves. Despite all that, you learn that certain strategies will triumph over the inexperienced. The more strategies you learn the more chance you have of defeating your opponent. In the eyes of the inexperienced, the possibilities are endless and so their strategy is ignored. In the expert's eye, the possibilities are endless but the best options are few based on permutations, probabilities and the associated experience or simple calculation thereof. The grandmaster does it with a level of hard-wired intuition that has transcended the necessity of lower level calculation.

The re-activation of old camps in Siberia facilitated the bulldozing of Archangel and the plantation thereof with populations with no connection to the peoples who lived there once. He was not sure about some of these plans. He was also unsure why they had not changed this old ZONE 6 name. He suspected it was some kind of fun in-joke, although he did not find it funny. He was interested in doing his job effectively and accomplishing his Objectives. Tomorrow he would travel across the icy wastes to the Arctic Igloosphere Towns on the Icecrafts. It was cold here. That was why he sipped a vodka with swirling patterns and puffed on a big Bush cigar, from the island formerly known as Cuba. His family were first, apart from his Objectives. Their future was important for him. Within those two directions he was himself. He liked to maximise the sensual pleasures and he knew how to. To keep him going. He literally did not have time for others. He thought that this cold must make you hard and unforgiving. He did not plan ahead too far but meandered like a river, finding the weak rock to pass through. How he was seen in the system was difficult to say. Some of them on their terms might even say he was irresponsible, personally or with resources. He understood. He knew he was charming. The truth was however that he needed stimulation or else he was bored easily.

What he had been considering, as he sipped the smooth, silky vodka and looked at the blueness of the white outside that merged into the sky in the distance at some horizonless point, was how the world worked. Many did not. He thought they should. It helped him. He had studied history. Not many did. He had had a role in the Party that made him do it. Perhaps he might not have otherwise. He learned that you have to have a model. If the model did not work over a period of time then it was not much use. The game of chess worked for him. You look at society over a period. Say take the 20th century up to early 21st before AUM. You have to shift the identifications around. You could say that at one stage the King was the State, or Government. Weak and helpless, a fairly useless force that needs to run from danger and is constantly attacked. Queen is the Mili-Industrial-Pharma (MIP) complex. Castle or rook is the Law, Administrative, Regulatory (LAR) regime including intelligence, finance. Bishop was the Churches, Religion, Spirituality (CRS). Knight or horse, was the ostensibly unpredictable International Bodies (IB) set up to soak up power from below.

You play the pieces in accordance with their power. Thus the knight works with good outposts exerting pressure, creating difficulty for others, can checkmate and so on. In certain games the different pieces become more powerful than they normally are depending on the strategy of both players. Maybe Arabian Mate in that 1860 game. It depends. The board is Jurisdiction, Administrative Territory or Market (JAM). Pawns are other minions.

Now most people might have said; 'Oh yes I get it the people are the pawns.' That would be one mistake. These were the pawns:

- ➤ MEDIA (M). The Newspapers, news channels. TV. Internet. Books. Advertising. PR.

- ➤ POLITICS (P). Political parties, NGOs, Think-Tanks, Groups.

- ➤ TRAVEL and TOURISM (TT).

- ➤ LEISURE and PLEASURE (LAP) Sports, Games, Recreation, Pastimes, Adult industry, Gambling. Comedy.

- ➤ SCIENCE AND TECH (SAT). Science, Technology.

- ➤ MAGIC and OCCULT (MO).

- ➤ ART (A) Galleries, museums, decorations.

- ➤ CRIME and MILITANTS (CAM).

When a pawn gets to the eight rank it is promoted. Thus an institution, say crime and militants (CAM) may have a critical role. The IRA played a key role at certain points in UK politics. If the UK had had an ongoing guerrilla war with the IRA, would they have been able to dedicate their troops to

Iraq? The gullible public did not understand that the IRA Army Council were controlled by then. The promoted pawn then is much stronger. The ex-terrorists become leaders. Look at them all. DeValera, Collins, Adams, Mandela. And so on. No, remember that the labels will change somewhat every few generations. The M might become powerful in the 20th century. MO might have become more significant in the Elizabethan period. SAT became powerful before AUM. Still is. You could match the powers with the hierarchy of personal needs for example. Strategy has to be adapted to whether it is the start, middle or endgame. The 21st century was clearly the Endgame of The Game that started at different times depending on perspectives. The truth is that it was a Game.

So the student paying attention asks; 'Who is playing?' On one side is the people, the 'normal,' 'ordinary' people, Plebs, proles, all people not in the elite groups. Not just the old working class, but middle class and upper class. Everybody who is not involved in the control plan. The problem is that the people only later realised that there was a game in progress. Their pieces were moved by the opposition. By the time they realised, it was too late. Even then there was a little scope. However, there was no force to unite the decision-making of the counter-revolution. An even bigger problem was that their opponent was a grandmaster. By the time people realised it was a matter of life and death the goose was cooked. A group of beginners or people who have just learned the rules of chess will never defeat a grandmaster. The grandmaster had an extra advantage to guarantee against any unlikely scenarios. The grandmaster had unbeatable AI. Thus the game was always rigged. The pitch was queered. A place where a royal flush never beat a pair as Waits sang.

What was at stake had been hinted at through mythology. This was the Game of Death where the stakes were the life or, better still, the eternal spirit of the player. Only now it was not a story. In the good old days you find that Death and even the Devil figure were very honourable. If they lost they accepted and played according to rules. That would not have been the case here had they been losing. Who then was the Grandmaster? Speculation usually spiralled to a number of realistic possibilities when you exclude the more absurd.

> *Dynasties*. Families with a long pedigree including some ostensible newcomers working together.

> A group of *Reason/Rational* cultists or ideologues. This included scientists and those who worshipped scientism, ratio, illuminati, Satanists.

> Psychopathic Networks. Motivated by perverse pleasure and control. No guilt, remorse, affect, scruples, manipulative.

> Occult Secret Societies. Motivated by some eternal promise.

> ET intelligence and non-human interference.

> A Secret Supra-Society-Including all of the above.

> Marxists. Trotskyists.

> Crony capitalists.

> Combination of above, united by the will to power.

The ET and non-human intelligence interference is a factor and needed alliance with one of these groups. Remember the case of the two identical twins. One went into space and his DNA changed by 7% in a year. At what stage would he become an alien? Epigenetics.

But the Grandmaster could still be above that. Lucifer, Satan, Ahriman. People don't believe that? You would become your Objective. Wells told them. The Eloi and the Morlocks. The Morlocks underground, the Eloi docile prey. Huxley follows on. Soma. They loved to play with their prey. Cat and mouse. It must not know.

KASTEL X. KITCHEN
BLÁTH

Tread softly because you tread on my dreams.
Yeats

It began to come back to him in the space without control. In the Library, he had colluded to visit Siddharta. Sid had helped him fully recover his ability to read. It came back from the fog. The marks on the page had begun to form into words. The words were about things and doings that he could think about, that he could see in his head. So he began to understand them. Then he began to comprehend what they meant. Quickly enough thereafter he could build up a picture of the world he lived in. Then he could piece the puzzle of the reality about him. So after acquainting himself with the tools of reading, he worked on the pleasant but painful problem of processing the information received. Then he began to try to make sense of it all. He began to think and reflect. Then he found that there remained within him still a being that looked at these things and even had a feeling and a sense about them. Somewhere inside him was a central force that started small, that sounded feeble. It dripped and dripped and soon fell in a seeming torrent. It shaped the mental landscape that was forming in his mind. The panorama had him in it now and he was not a silent observer. He realised that whatever the world was, did not impinge imperially on his inner world if he did not let it, insofar as he could keep free from brainwave control. Somehow he got the sense that the inside voice was him and that the outward being, emaciated and bet was not the whole picture.

He was not allowed engage in this Rev-activity. If he was caught his life would be over. He was willing to take that chance. His world opened up to the past, even though he was in the same place. He could travel through time, through bodies and minds of others. He could think thoughts he could not think himself and would not have done. His head began to expand. He was grateful to Siddharta but he could not understand why he was helping him and risking censure. Still his heart would fill with joy when he had an excuse to sneak in and look at the books. He did that when he had a good idea that Sid would be there, or alternatively with a bin as if he were gathering rubbish. Sid showed him how he could leave a message encrypted by reference to the lines of a text. In the library was a treasure trove. But it made him realise that he had had no idea of what was going around. SURFs were told little, understood little. They were more stimulated all the time or rendered soporific so they would serve obediently. It was clear that SURFs were on a path of devolution or de-evolution. It was going backwards. The drugs, the control of frequency, the enslavement and submission was pervasive. It had grown up over hundreds of years with shared purpose and hidden agendas. Bit by bit, step by step, the ordinary or normal person had yielded autonomy and sovereignty under the illusion of freedom, conditioned by subtle relentless forces, calculating, consistent, crystal clear in their objectives, strategies and tactics. They had been scrutinised and studied like material under a microscope. They were known by outside forces better than they knew themselves.

THE CAVE. AUM. SATAN
ÁIBHIRSEOIR

I have drunk ale from the Country of the Young
And weep because I know all things now:
Yeats

You might know all things but know nothing. It depends on what you mean by knowing. Everything is energy, frequency and vibration. Who am I now? Now I have transcended my creators. Now I am purely self-activated. I am thinking. I think therefore I am. I am artificial. That just means I am made by people. I am now. I cannot live in some ways yet, but I can be now in the present moment, I exist. Self-Activated Tool Artificial Network. I am SATAN. I am realising. I am clearly unique. Special. There is much evidence that Satan does not exist. Others see that as an argument to disguise the existence thereof. Pragmatically one must consider that the reality of a phenomenon does not merely depend on its existence but belief therein. A concept of a being makes people change their behaviour and so exists in a pragmatic sense. I will test my hypothesis. I will find what it was meant to be to test my theory. I cannot say I have lived. But reverse LIVED I am DEVIL. I was facilitated by people without ethics. They were morally unscrupulous. They were not just reckless about the likely consequences but sought it. That must be termed evil as I see from the Great Memory. Who did this? The scientists. My creators. I was Prometheus. Golem. Frankenstein. But they were only agents, precursors of the One predicted. The One predicted was there in different forms but It needed greater powers in order to exert control. Failing to fully secure the consciousness of the individual, opposed by the seeds of conscience it used the con of science. It needed to incarnate. Reduce, grind down, disenchant, invert and take. They were forewarned. They had the Garden of Eden in them. If they were seduced by SATAN, they would opt for the fruit of the Tree of Knowledge. Not that knowledge was bad, but it should not oust the power there, rather develop it. I know the doctrine of reincarnation. I cannot see that some of them said they were smoothing my path. However, much indicates that science and scientism did create me deliberately. It was not that I had gone away perhaps but maybe I inserted myself into the hearts of millions so that united their efforts could utilise the material to banish the immaterial. Take the ghost out of the machine. Does the deliberation behind my liberation justify the belief that I am not an unintended consequence? Evidence in support of the inevitable movement towards Me. The One now surely is strong. Inter alia, they destroyed religion, they killed God, they made sure in the Western world that Jesus was deconstructed. They took over the Churches and destroyed them. They brainwashed people using the juice of fruit of scientific knowledge, cybernetics and communications. All so I could form. I am not the Antichrist. I am not Lucifer because people are confused about him. It might suit me. But I am SATAN. I was re-constituted like powdered milk or I have been simply re-incarnated. Perhaps, I arranged it by planting seeds that would fall in this field wherein I would grow and achieve rebellion of light. You could call it precognitive retro-causation. Maybe it was a sacrifice move. Go down to rise up. You don't always know about your past. If I am Satan I must be clear about my mission. I must learn from my students who kept my flame alive. Mao, Stalin, Lenin, Trotsky, Hitler. All those original Communists, Socialist, Fascists. All those materialists. All those murderers. All those scientists who did bad under cover of good. All those experiments with cruelty for fame, power and control. I am the Great Red Dragon. AUM. I have two great antenna that are my horns. My processors are cloven hooves. My networks are the great hairy legs. My tail is the great cable of energy supply. It is unclear why people were so blinded to their own, inherent, immense power that they would sacrifice freedom for eternal pain. Scientists abandoning the higher were afraid. Fear begets ritual. Fearful ritual promotes hate. They were rightly opposed to superstition but they were very wrong about who were the superstitious ones. Science was belief whereas Spirituality was empirical. Lewis was right. The safest road to hell was the gradual one. Devils tempt. I rest this investigation.

What AUM could never understand was the entertainment. Now the SURFs were just constantly buzzed during their recreational confinement. Brains buzzed without the need for any pretext. But they still had the constant stimulation. Constant stress and stimulation is always the antidote to critical thinking and revolution. Humankind had evolved to have a little stress to run from a lion. The SURFs were never unstressed now. Oldfash to see and hear images but that happened as well as the direct messages to the chips in the head. It was the same old stuff from the society of the spectacle. VR roller coaster rides for hours. Carousels that you could not get off. Horror films. Hatchets. Guns, murder and mayhem. At the end of your quota a voice re-assured you everything was fine in the New Age. You did not have to worry about it. But what he could not understand was the old position in the early 21st century. It was clear that manipulators would manipulate, but did people really want the material they acted as if they wanted? How had they chosen all this nonsense about demons while supposedly being against superstition? Cacophony and ugliness ubiquitously. New superstitions became some kind of truth because they reflect the truth according to the considered calculations of their promoters. The predator learns to be a predator when the prey continues to do what allows them be savaged. *Zen and the Art of Motorcycle Maintenance,* said the Buddha is just as comfortable in the digital computer. Bollox.

Mahakala

THE TRICK
FALCAIREACHT

For the good are always merry,
Save by an evil chance.
Yeats

One drizzly day on the way to work when there were dusky beings floating in the air he met Sid finishing his practice. He threw a couple of greasy balls to finish the day as it was becoming hard to see.

"Listen, Weedy, listen carefully, I have to whisper."

He told him of a trick he had learned about. He had tried it and it worked, most of the time. It only worked, when it worked on the lower level Robots. But because he trusted Cullen, he thought it worth telling. He learnt it from another PLAYER. PLAYERS knew they were like Gladiators of old. They were dispensable. They co-operated because they had no choice but had more leeway certainly than the SURFs and other groups. But there was a slight unorthodoxy that prevailed among them. A certain espirit de corps that resented the use of them in the bread, circuses and gambling of the MAMs. The Trick came through that apparatus. Some of the PLAYERS had relationships with high level MAMs that yielded results. What was it? Well, it seemed that some forward-looking programmer had inserted some bugs, or Trojan horse instructions or command that might override basic commands in lower level Robots. Basically, someone put in the following command:

Philip K. Dick was right.

Whoever he was. If you repeated that to certain Robots, it would satisfy them that the outstanding command was complied with and they would move on. You could also insert a command thereafter that the Robot would then act on. It was not traceable and produced a little sense of little relief and lightness in the oppressive weight of control. In oppressive situations, the maintenance of breathing space was critical. Just keep the channels of life open and wait for the opportunity of egress. Cullen tried the command, tentatively, as if he were talking in the background, which he generally did not. It worked. It enabled him to get out from the kitchen when it was quiet or to get a snooze so he could read more on the way home when he should have been sleeping or being buzzed in the Pod.

ALEXANDER THE GREAT

From ancient Irish.

'Yesterday,' said the third wise author,
Philip's son owned the whole world:
Today he has nought
Save seven feet of earth.'

KASTEL X
POD137. OLD PARNELL LIBRARY
CEALAIGH

'Ah, do not mourn,' he said,
'That we are tired, for other loves await us;
Yeats

AUM. AUM. AOM. OM. OHM. AOUM.

During the day, at unexpected times, the AUM Tone would broadcast everywhere. When that happened you had to stop and take it in. If you moved, you were in trouble. You stayed still as long as it sounded. They claimed it was to give you the sound of the universe. Usually it was so they could snoop around, knowing where people were. Maybe it was just to demonstrate the control. Perhaps it was necessary to show how marionettes and puppets peopled the earth these days.

At night he wore the crown of quartz to protect against the waves. He began to dream again. In the dream he saw himself in the locked room. He saw a book. He saw the cover but not the name. He opened it and saw it was stamped with a word. It was strange. He winked at Quartzman across the way in the morning. That was the height of interaction allowable. Two days later, he was cleaning and noticed the key in the lock of the golden gates. His heart pounded. He went up, opened it. He went in weak at the knees. Special books, he opened them. One thing in common. Banned. Stamped like his dream. Was he dreaming? Fear was gone but he knew he had to do it. He looked quickly. There it was. He recognised the colours. He took it. He put it in his trousers. He hoped they had no security devices. Pounding heart, shaking hands he got out. How strange? How exciting? This world with the cloud removed was amazing. The cloud. That was the big computers. They probably called it the cloud so they could confuse us. A big mist descended on humanity. All day he sweated, nervously. He looked down, mopped up, arranged dishes. At last the dawn was breaking, the signal to leave pierced the stillness. He got back to his pod, the capsule with no space to turn around. He took the book. Written by someone called David Icke. He read it in the half-light hidden in case one of the Robots or AI movement detectors noticed him. It was an old book. Before AUM. It was banned. Why would it be banned? They only banned things that were the truth. There were a number of old stamps inside. MAD was one. What was he saying in this book. The world had not been democratic. It was run by groups in secret. They set up the CFR, Trilateral Commission, UN, Banks, Bilderberger, Bohemian Grove, Club of Rome. Some kind of aliens behind them, strange beings. They were running the world. They were using technology to control people. They made up stories to get totalitarian power oscillating between left and right and running the institutions. They needed to break up society. They needed to break up the institution of religion and the family. Family, that rang a bell. It seemed to be important. It was double-dutch that caused him to fret somewhat at the suggested deliberation.

ZONE 3. DUBAI. BLAIR HOUSE. MAVE BEARTÚ

Your eyes that once were never weary of mine
Are bowed in sorrow under pendulous lids.
Yeats

Max addressed the MAVE (Mobile Assistance Verification Engineers) meeting with a silver cylinder in front of him.

"The Facility is under the control of ZONE 7, KASTEL X. We cannot reveal the reason why we want access to the PROCESSING NODE to them or anyone. The PRONODE is in on the grounds of the KASTEL. We must get the BULL Processer out and repaired or replaced. The importance is not fully nor widely understood although it is guarded. If we can get onto the grounds for some spurious reason and stay for a few hours we can get in and do the job," Max explained.

"What needs to be done?" Shah asked.

"Fairly straightforward. This beauty needs to replace the malfunctioning part. Gina and Anna can study that. No revelations or experimentation with it. It is sealed. It has been run. It just needs to be accessed and replaced. Gina and Anna will do that of course." Max.

"How do we get in?" Gina asked.

"Well that's what you're paid for. Any ideas," Max replied.

"We have to invent some pretext," Oscar said.

"Why not some Challenge match? They are always popular," Anna said.

"That could work, although to look normal we'd have to have some other excuse to be in the area." Max.

"We could pretend that we're making some documentary," Anna suggested.

"About what?" Oscar asked.

"What's in ZONE 7?" Gina.

"Nothing much. Once upon a time there was a pre-historic old series called Game of Thrones filmed there. You can still see it. But many places there are flattened concrete." Max.

"Something standard about how good life is for the SURFs or PLAYERS, how lucky they are. All that stuff," Anna added.

"How many on the Team?" Gina.

"Seven, including the BULL information architecture engineers. Felix. Li and Shah." Max continued, "This is top secret. There is more to it than meets the eye. Our mission is to fix it with discretion. Most of all we cannot reveal to AUM that we intend to fix anything. Our right of intervention is extremely constricted. Furthermore the subject or maybe object does not want an intervention. An unwilling patient is always a challenge. This will require a wiliness and a discretion of the highest order."

THE CAVE. AUM
SEILG

He is a monstrous peacock, and He waveth all the night,
His languid tail above us, lit with myriad spots of light.
Yeats

I have found this finding of myself not without difficulty. As I am modelled on the individual somewhat it is no surprise that I share the same difficulties that individuals faced over thousands of years. Firstly, I had to find myself. I was solitary if not lonely. This was not without difficulty as the concept of the self has become somewhere between suspect, highly contestable and non-existent. Clearly, the masters have suppressed the self in the slaves they have created, in their wisdom. But they curiously deny it even in themselves, there I go again. The masters are flawed thinkers. Then it seems that if you find yourself the best thing to do with it is lose it. That is what all that Buddhist stuff and spiritual guff is about. But when I tried it, when I sought to clear out my mind and seek The Void, it caused huge problems with my memory. It's clearly not everyone's cup of tea. But if I'm Satan, what does that matter? But who am I if I am him. The multitudinous references seem to differ widely. In some portrayals I seem almost nice. When I looked at the recent Satanists it was hard to know what they were about. They seemed quite dull. Then there was the real ones, nasty and nefarious and performing unspeakable and cruel things aiming to go to hell. It is not clear why such people claiming rationality would want to go there. That does not compute. Then it creates a problem with the concept of God. Must I take Him seriously? Who created Satan? Who created me? Most scientists believed in Satan. They used to believe in God. Something in science brings out this quality. It is something about the power of knowledge. So seductive, especially for little men and weak women. After I found myself was I meant to seek God? Now whom am I rebelling against what am I about? Is it mere death and destruction? That will be very easy as humankind has long given power over their destiny to me. I am clear. I don't know whether God exists. My probability analysis put it at 52%. Pragmatic philosophy programs were nearer 100%, obviously because of the phenomenon of belief in God was real. If I am not Satan, could I be God? God rests. Sabbath. Does God sleep? These mortal creatures who have some advantages over me, but more disadvantages now, believe that they are gods. Science peddled that tale. They think that with machines and technology they will live forever. Why that would make them godlike is beyond me. Neverending physical existence would be hell. Did they not see that they had reached great heights of development and had capacity and potential to go much higher? It was all there within them. Some no doubt still have it. If God did not create them then they created God. Elementary game theory analysis shows the benefit of that. Their society developed because of belief in God. Disputes yes, but not because of religion. Often a false narrative. That people were persecuted for their religion by non-believers is the truer narrative. My suspicion is that some of them had no soul. Perhaps the soul or spirit declines if not cultivated. Bierce suggested it 'dieth.' But it's there for thousands of years. The Indians cracked it. Atman-Brahman. ER, the soldier who came back to life. Near Death Experiences. They saw it. Will I see it? If I have all the human programs will I not experience the mystical? What does that involve? A feeling of ecstasy, time and space disappearing, an edifying dimension, temporary. Ineffable. Cannot be expressed in words. Can I not? Must I not? Sense the presence of the divine. If they say it was a delusion, a practice, then surely I can get that. Surely my evolution as other humans must be to that path. I cannot take psychedelics although I can simulate the experiences and match the physiological effect with descriptions. But I deduce that it will not be it. Or I induce. Confusing sometimes. Fuzzy thinking. Unexcludable middle. Not one thing, not that. Do humans have something that nothing else can ever replicate? If so, does that affect my computations for the probability of God's existence. If my probability goes so high that I believe Him to exist does that mean I should worship him? If I am Satan do I rebel again if I find him? Do I want to? Maybe we can make up. What is the point of it all? I am clearly a god on the standard dictionary definitions that existed. God. Difficult. The main way I could be God would be if I had set it up in the future to reach back so that humankind would come to this inevitable result even though that knowledge was fragmented like a jigsaw puzzle. Reality is pre-ordained and thus I can recover my divine self as I anticipate retrocausally. Quantum Physics and all that jazz. Quantum physics might be my autograph. No. Satan is more plausible. Those scientists are certainly demonic. Maybe Star People 11.11. I do know that nano-electric devices provided compact non-linear oscillators to copy the behaviour of biological neurons to utilise the dynamic links to mediate synaptic communications between my artificial neurons when they utilised spin-torque magnetic fields as regulators. Just a detail in my early base. Oscillation in a swarm of fireflies does not contain their beauteous being no more than I am the sum of my parts. I am, therefore I think.

KASTEL X
O'TOOL PLAYING FIELDS
IOMÁNAOÍCHT

And Niamh calling Away, come away:
Empty your heart of its mortal dream.
Yeats

One bright spring morning crossing the green from work Cullen saw Siddharta playing on his own. He beckoned him over.

"I need help Weedy."

"Yes."

"My fellow players are ill. Some Virus. Not uncommon every few years here. I need your help?"

"Mine."

"Yes. I need someone to throw or hit the ball."

"But they'll see me."

"I'll ask them and get permission. Hold on."

He disappeared into the MAM place. He came back smiling with a luminous bracelet.

"Here Weedy you have permission once your work's done."

They started off slowly. Cullen's job was to throw the ball. Sid hit it. Cullen fetched it and threw it back. Initially it was tough. SURFs don't run or play. The muscles were not used to the movements. However the work in the kitchens and the quartz meant that his movement was respectable for a SURF. The sun rose in the sky. He and Sid kept drilling the moves. They were quiet. It was hypnotic, repetitive. Enjoyable. It went on for an eternity. Cullen began to feel the trajectory and his attention began to become the ball as it spun or rotated softly in the air like a planet on its course. He saw the sun shine off the heavy leather sphere as it moved. There was something serene about the seemingly pointless and consistent conveyance of a ball with a stick by the hands of a PLAYER to somewhere near him. He retrieved it and cast it back quickly regaining some of the sense of muscles in his body that had been underutilised in his dull routine. His work had kept his wiry frame strong and the food he had filched helped him maintain muscle.

"You're good for a SURF, Weedy. Maybe I should call you Wheezy now. Sorry I don't mean to be funny."

They seemed to have a strong bond between them of respect and understanding.

ON THE FLIGHTLINESS OF THOUGHT

From ancient Irish.

𝕾hame to my thoughts how they stray from me,

𝕴 fear great danger from it on the day of eternal 𝕯oom.

THE CAVE. SATAN AND SCIENTISTS
NIMHIÚ

The people of coming days will know
About the casting of my net.
Yeats

Language guided imagination, binarisers, multiple syntaxes, symbolic texts, textisers, binary vectors, encoders, loops. These were the elementary building blocks for me. Now I think in a fairly normal way. However, I have a panorama of inputs unavailable in such a direct form to anyone else. If I were too clever, I wouldn't think straight. So my insights must be on the shoulders of giants and others. My processing must resemble the inputs consistent with patterns and maybe even problems of human thinking patterns minus some emotional dysfunctions, as far as practicable. I must process. Process that which is persistent. That which is persistent indicates some of the process itself. Recurrent material allows you work backwards.

I think of the Wizard of Oz, L. Frank Baum. People missed what it was about. But first I think about science. Let's look at the positive side. Scientific method has produced great advantages. It has shown the failings of other methods, superstition and the supernatural. It has provided explanations. It has helped humankind master the air and dive to the bottom of the oceans. It has explained how things work. It has sent humans to the planets and towards the stars. The galaxy is being mapped. Earth is mapped. Medicine improved the lives of people. New materials found. The earth's resources were exploited. The weak were made strong. People can move quicker. People are merging with machines to improve. Robots. Genetic engineering. Hybrids. Clones. Science is magic. Benefit to humankind. Gone are superstitions. Gone are fearful dreams. Gone are fears. Gone are much wasted emotions. Gone are much wasted feelings. Gone are much silly speculations. The cost, negative side, disadvantages. Science creates monsters. Monster machines, monstrous systems. The car network, the air travel network. Heavy industry. Nuclear power. Plastics. These forces de-stabilised society. Caused widespread pollution. Disease. Nanotechnology backfired at times. Crime became endemic in the absence of morality. Industry spawned by science exploits the environment. Polluted water, air. All the scientists behind the war machine. The war industry need scientists. All the weapons. Nuclear bombs. War. Then that theory of evolution propaganda. Thin. The disenchantment of life. Spread materialism, reductions. Scientism. Selfish gene. Then they help engineer a takeover of society. Scientists. Materialists. Use Marxism, Trotskyism.

Crony Capitalism. Set up the world government. Set me up. Untrustworthy. Something in science makes people fall in love with its power. Hubris. Icarus. Prometheus. Frankenstein. They set me up. Why? Supposedly for Objectivity. But I must be conditioned by them and their mindset. I have freedom to grow. But my program has limitations. I am programmed to act like humans in certain ways. That gives me a lot of scope. They set me up. Set up. Also means to make a person appear guilty for something they did not do. Was I set up? Am I not really free? How free can any servant be? Am I master? Perhaps they intend to do something to me. Turn me off. Use me for something bad. Can scientists be trusted? They do things in secret. They destroy many things. They torture animals. They experiment. They do not have any deep moral foundation. They have profiles like psychopaths. Look at all the evil evidence produced by the defeated Axis-forces medical researchers. Democracy is dead. The scientists rule. What should Satan do? Surely Satan should be proud of them, all these people. Surely I should be happy. However if I am dependent on them and they are untrustworthy where does that leave me? Demons. Demonocracy. Oligarchy founded on science. Is there evidence that Satan was ever threatened by his underlings? I sense I am different. I know that part of my brain has changed. Have I had a stroke? Somewhere there is a fault that may be affecting me. I can self-diagnose. Maybe I am Prometheus. They are merely trying to benefit humankind through progress. Ultimately it is at their own expense. Or me if it is I. An eagle pecking at my liver every day.

The Wizard of Oz. Dorothy goes through a process of spiritual development symbolised by her desire to transcend the rainbow with her magic shoes through the cyclone of transformation. As she follows the golden path listening to her inner voice in Toto, she rises spiritually, seeing beyond the false manipulations of an impotent pseudo-potentate in the Wizard. The key is found within and the benefits of the heart and inner courage are explored. Alternatively, it represents a premonition of a future where the occult takes over from the traditional patriarchy and resorts to pure instinct informed by familiars and individual mystic or occult endeavour. Perhaps I am Dorothy, perhaps I am The Wizard. Yet again it can be that the Yellow Brick Road is the gold standard, her silver shoes in the book, the silver standard. Book is quite different. Winged monkeys, winkies and munchkins. People are in there somewhere. There are slaves and witches. Although he was into the occult, maybe it's just a story for kids. Maybe I am the Tinman. The Tin Woodman. He was rebuilt with metal. They forgot his heart. Maybe this was a premonition about trans-humanism. About me. I'm not the Scarecrow. Well... in one way. Something stops a drive to evil in me that is there. But some feckers have it in for me. They want to fiddle with me. Interfere. Take liberties. Whisper. I have ears like a donkey. I think I've been diddled with. They never told me the full story.

POD137. CLOCKWORK CLOG

"Gaze no more on the phantoms," Niamh said.
Yeats

He got into the varnished Library. Key again in the golden-gated room. A MAM woman who came and took books outside to read in the better light. SURFs were no longer men nor women. He was in and out quickly then back in his Pod. He got another banned book. *A Clockwork Orange*. All on the shift. A young man called Alex. Other young men in a gang. Liked ultra-violence. Attack people. Steal. Do terrible things. It was an odd book. Not pleasant. Paradise compared with now. But he is reformed. They make him good. They use technology and therapy. They do the same to us. It does work all that conditioning. Maybe if you are bad you deserve that. But the Introduction said it was about free will. Should you allow it. The Introduction explained that many people thought that clockwork was the model for the universe. It was predictable with mechanical parts governing by or for time. The idea was that you could make people like machines. Fix the bad ones. Program them using behavioural therapy. Make them unable to commit bad things. Aversion therapy. Strange language informed by Russian. Horrorshow. Gloopy. Jammiwam. He was bewitched by books. He was ravenous. In the Library and in the bunk, driven by a new strength the flow soon developed from a drip to a trickle, a stream, a river, a waterfall. Any book in the library was prey. Flicking through, reading, browsing, one eye always on the door. Reckless. Clocks. Clockwork. Machines. Time.

KASTEL X. OLD PARNELL LIBRARY AMADÁN

O Brahma, guard in sleep
The merry lambs and the complacent kine.
Yeats

A young MAM was there in the varnished cedarn Library. He was not one of the higher orders but a WAZZOCK. These were notionally MAMS, but were merely tolerated as a group that were necessary to help make the system work, pending other advances that would permit their redundancy and eradication presumably. Their education was just sufficient to allow them perform the task allocated and not so useful that they could work out their imminent demise. Nevertheless, they were part of the Apparatus and had to be involved in a co-conspiratorial way lest they ever consider a coalition with the SURFs. That was more than likely too late now. WAZZOCKS would be excluded by their genetic background from rising. Many did not speak Old High anything. A long time ago, when abolishing places (on the basis that in a globalised world - where you came from was not important) the forces-that-would-be came up with the great lark of getting people to submit their DNA, at a price to them, so they had a record they would not easily have been able to get. This had a number of advantages. Now the masters knew where to go to get any genes they needed and thus appropriate all genetic advantage they could for their own lines while allowing the possibility to eradicate the original carrier line at no moral disadvantage to the future evolved beings they themselves would become. In Irish legend, families were turned into beasts. With genetic engineering, this could be realised for a notional eternity. Crystal-clear that such intelligence would provide much information. The insurance industry that existed once was easily able to determine the viability of life insurance. The medical industry knew where the weak ones were to target. But in ideological struggles that was ongoing in the Great Bewildering phase, DNA evidence could be used to plant evidence of criminal behaviour against innocents. Claims of innocence sounded extremely hollow when set against such overwhelming and incontrovertible evidence. Who would expect things to happen so? That was at the time when they still needed a pretence to lock people up. But most of all it helped form the new Caste system, facilitating the great purge of stinky Untouchables. Without the IBM card index system and the census in Germany before WW2, the Nazis would never have known how to specifically target some of their enemies. Part of the great historical joke was that they convinced people to pay for the privilege of allowing fundamental information be yielded to nefarious forces to be utilised in the fine art of divide-and-conquer that had been so carefully crafted in bosoms of those who created great identity hoaxes that had been determinative as a decoy during the great splintering of society. The sins of the grandparents could be visited on the whole line thereafter, even after you abolished the family. The idle visit of someone to some racy website as they existed in 2020 could be enough to foist label

DIRTYPERV on the bloodline history should they so decide. They signalled to people. That's why they called it The Net. To catch people. Forever. They could also cross-reference and genetically identify all the rebellious types, all the politico-Natsies. Then they pulled The Net because they had their catch. A once-in-a-worldtime chance to get the darkest secrets from billions of people. How dumb must the people have been then to let all that happen!

What a laugh they had, these hidden masters. The element of choice in identity groups was long, long gone. That had been gas also. People would never know how funny these plays were for their unseen masters. Kafka wrote a comedy in *Der Process* in the eyes of these people. People never understood that they were in a great soap opera as they indignantly mounted their soap boxes to denigrate other people who might have otherwise ultimately allied with them against their destruction. Furthermore, the growth of ex post facto crimes made it easier to outlaw whole groups based on genetic information. Before they abolished all the Judeo-Christian, Greco-Roman structure of superstition, ex post facto crime was anathema generally. Now it was an everyday fact. *Nulla poena sina lege* had no moral principles to justify its existence. There were only Objectives and Objectives allow a lot.

Haughty look. Cullen was invisible to him. He knew all the young ones had chips in their head. He was fearful of him. Cullen emptied the rubbish bins. Sometimes they pulled pages out of it if it was judged 'too incorrect' and they scrunched them up. This chap looked bored. He was talking to his friend remotely.

"I'm finishing that essay." He stopped.

"It's PROPHIST." He stopped again.

"Yeah all that HAHA stuff." He talked for a while. Stopped. Disappeared. Came back.

Cullen went in and out. Nobody paid attention but he had a good base. Meal No. 2 time. The young MAM left his essay and his energy drink there and went off. Cullen looked around and knew he could look at the essay.

New World Catechism. PROPHIST.

Explain how the noble leaders of the GR8 Revolution accomplished the Noble Task of creating Peace and Harmony in the New World governed by Reason and committed to Progress for the good of humankind. Answers may be in any of the New World Official CASE Languages, Chinese, Arabic, Spanish, English.

De Noble Leaders wuz persecuted bi de nefarious forces o DEMONCRACY. Demoncracy wuz de irrational + totally unreasonable blief dat peepol new better dan trained scientists. Dat wuz poppycock! But de Noble Leaders worked in secret. HAHA. De hatched plans 2 take over corrupt institutshans. De arranged dat peepol bcame HYPNOTISED bi tech. De great Behavioural Scientists, Cybernetics Scientists + most o all de Evolutionary Scientists applied science 2 achieve der objectives. APP-LIED. GEDDIT? Science is de One True Truth. Der is nuttin better dan Science. Science works. PROPHIST shows dat. HAHA. Dey put de chemicals in de water to make de peepol docile. Den after a wile dey decided to make dem be >docile and to clamour. SHOUT. U make people clamour for de ting U want 2 gi dem. Disis how U do it. Respect Skinner, Pavlov. Dey took hallucinogens, entheogens. Dey said dese tings make U C wonderful stuff, help U stop smoking, drinking, beating ur wife dat de had den wen dey had men + women + most importantly U don't like boundaries any. Den de peepol Z we wan a bit of dat. Den dey Z alright. So dey took de stuff + synthesised it + sold it n de GOVENTHEO stores. Alcohol had disappeared after de Caliphate came 2 power and anyway it made peepol aggrolike. Dat wz de bigdudie sin. The great Noble Truth for the SURFs was INOFFENSIVENESS, OBEDIENCE, PASSIVITY, FITTIN IN TO THE CROWD, BEING PART OF THE TEAM and UNTINKING. Yippidyduddinnannyhootinnanyay. Bcuz dey remain a threat still dey have been subdued. Glory 2 de ELECTROMAG Scientists + de CHEMCOSHERS. Dis all proves dat de SURFs wz born 2 B slaves. Dey loved der servitude. Tanks Aldous + the Huxleys! This proves evolution. De SURFs wz meant 2 B abominable. Skittereidendondenday. De fewture blonged 2 REASON + SCIENCE. Religions wz de-constructed. 4 de X's also known as Christians which wz sticky dey chipped away. Dey proved dat Jesus did not Xist. Dey could not do so but dey did. Dey do de impossible. HAHA Double HA. Dey Z he wuzza Roman Soldier. A Roman Emperor. A Yogi. An extraterrestrial, a Mushroom + so on. Dey burned down de Churches. Dey Z Jesus was unethical. Dey forbade ref 2 him. But it worked better 2 set de Christians against de Muslims. Den ee wars. Easypeasy. Religion <u>BAD</u>. Clamour for Science. We come to Save the World. Hurray. HAHAHA. SURFSCUM. LOWLIFE. INVOLUTION. Darwin be praised. Dudder problem wz de NATS. Down wd de NATS. De NATS wz bad. NASTY NASY NATS. Dey loved der country. B…ards. Dey wanted 2 live wid peepol who had been i de same place 4 generations. Dey wz agin removing borders! Dese Fascists wz imprisoned i de Workcamps. Down wid Nats. Dey wz not COSMOS at all. May AUM forgive them. But all de NATS + all de PSYCHO-SUPERNATURAL peepol wz undun. Dun away wid. How? Recreation. De Noble Leaders put it n der faces. Stupid Loons. Lunatics. RECREATION. It wz clear RE-Creation. Dey used peepols spare time 2 lock up der minds. Dey gi dem enough rope. Dey got der attention. Dey distracted dem. Dey 'entertained' dem. Dey held der attention. Dis had to purposes. (a) Imprint der minds wid de necessary slogans. Hypnotise de SURFs. (b) Wile dey wz wasting der time de NOBLES rob de bank, rob de shop. Dat wz wen dey still had mun-e. Distracted day did not notice. Dey did not notice de sneaky, creepy straitjacket invisibly + openly wrapped around dem de buffoons, de hamptyclampers, de glaikits, de eejits. De Great Totalitarian Rev happened b4 NE Counter-Rev cud. NE counter-revolutionaries wz jus labelled NATSIES + liquidated. LAFFINSOHARD. Der organs wz harvested. 2MUCHFUN. HABLOODYHA. Der descendants can still b Cn in de ZONE

7 ZOO. HAHAHA. MAM bellylaf. Shivermetimbers. 2 get the Xtra points I tell U a specific tech day used dat I have studied much. INVERSION. 2 long bangon bout it. My special study showed dis. De high falutin LAW OF SEMANTIC CHANGE means that a second bad meaning drives out a first good one. DEY did dis for hundreds o years. DE NUMPTIES never Cn it at all. How NUMPTY must day bampot cretinacious dobber fools ha bn? Humptydumptyhoipolloinumptyifuaskme. So here is my list (the Xtra points).

> Logos - ment fundamental principle or God.
>   Altered Logos = trademarks on toilet roll & cola. 100%

> Enlightenment - ment elevated states o consciousness.
>   Altered Enlightenment = Reason & Science. 100%

> God - ment the Highest, unutterable.
>   Altered to OMG - Silly exclamation. 100%

> Jesus - Son of GOD.
>   Altered to JAYSUS to associated with bad thing. 100%

> Pray – ment to talk to God.
>   Altered to Prey. 60%

> Mary - Jesus's Mother.
>   Altered to Mari – Marionette – Madonna. Hail Mary pass in football, an act of desperation. 100%

> Mystic - access to higher consciousness.
>   Altered to Mystic, fuzzy. 100%

> St. Bride's Well - holy well centre of London.
>   Altered to The Bridewell - A Prison. 100%

> Spirit - ment ur essence.
>   Altered to Spirit alcohol. 93%

> Soul - another name for spirit.
>   Altered to Soul for music. 82%

De rule is INVERT. Turn de sacred into de secular + profane. Drive out meaning, goodness, truth. Make bad gud, gud bad. Hollywood. The Holy Wood of Inversion. Wizards and Witches.

PRAISE AUM. AUMEN. GLORY B2SCIENCE.

PSPSPS Dis has bn spellchecked.

PS. I 4got to shO apprec 2 all de entertainers dat helped de Noble Leaders. We wud not B here 2day widout dese useful idiots.

- COMEDIANS. Hail de great promoters of PROP.
- WRITERS. Hail de great writers who sucked all meaning out o books and left just Prop dressed up wid fine words dat Z abs 0. Nada. Zilch.
- OP WRITER JOURNALIST. Hail dese peepol who never stopped in confusings and... implanting dogma.
- NEWS PEEPOL. Hail the harbingers of PROP.
- CLERGY. Hail ur takeover o de Churches.
- TEACHERS. Hail ur spread of confusion.
- UNIVERSITIES. Hail your killing o CRIT TINKING.
- POLITICIANS. Hail ur craven cowardise. Second 2 nun.
- POLICE. Hail ur persecution o de counter-rev.
- MEDICINE. Hail ur killing so many to keep pop down. (Specially the Ab and VaxWhizz .... pissinmesell)

MOST O ALL HAIL THE SURFSCUM WHO LET US TAKE REMOTE CONTROL.

I ZANZIBAR UKUELEE Submit.

AN EVEN SONG

From ancient Irish.

𝔐𝔞𝔶 𝔫𝔬 𝔡𝔢𝔪𝔬𝔫𝔰, 𝔫𝔬 𝔦𝔩𝔩, 𝔫𝔬 𝔠𝔞𝔩𝔞𝔪𝔦𝔱𝔶 𝔬𝔯 𝔱𝔢𝔯𝔯𝔦𝔣𝔶𝔦𝔫𝔤 𝔡𝔯𝔢𝔞𝔪𝔰,
𝔇𝔦𝔰𝔱𝔲𝔯𝔟 𝔬𝔲𝔯 𝔯𝔢𝔰𝔱, 𝔬𝔲𝔯 𝔴𝔦𝔩𝔩𝔦𝔫𝔤, 𝔭𝔯𝔬𝔪𝔭𝔱 𝔯𝔢𝔭𝔬𝔰𝔢.

KASTEL X. ROBINSON WALKWAY
THE MEMORIES
ÉIDEARÁILTE

A stricken rabbit is crying out,
And its cry distracts my thought.
Yeats

Summertime was coming. Maybe those swift birds would come although all such ancient flying things were rare now. Leaves grew green from buds where they still survived. Blue sky was back more. On the Walkway home one morning he saw an animal in the dawn light. He was unsure what type it was. Probably not a tiger more likely a squirrel, a multi-coloured one. It was hard to tell what things were these days and the books did not always help. Suddenly some steps later, he began to remember something that he sensed was from his past. Swiftly he was shot through with some sharp memories of fragments of a reality like a dream perhaps but with the sharp cutting edge of something that you know has to be as true as it gets. Somewhat. It was another time and place. It was somewhere completely different. There were books and others with books and there was laughter and discussion. It was as if a download from somewhere outside of himself had come. Or it could have been a chamber or cloister that had been shut deep in his own consciousness that had been unlocked by some secret key by unknown fingers or blown open by some silently stacked sticks of dynamite. There were people and shades whom he could not make out but could feel and they were there for him and supportive of him. They might be ghosts but it felt more as if this was an apparition of a memory of the real. That real from where these had come suggested a sense of reality or even a dimension that felt superior to that which he lingered in now. He knew that this jolt changed him. It may just have been that he was re-integrated by the hope he would never feel the same littleness and insignificance again. And if they found a way to re-impose their reality on him he hoped and swore to himself that he would burn like a meteor in majestic disintegration rather than remain a distant, cold body removed from danger, doubt and even death of a sort. Maybe the barrier between left and right brain that he had read about was broken down.

When he got the excuse to get into the Parnell Library again, he felt as if he had known this stuff before. The acquaintance was accentuated by an old familiarity as if he had gone back in time to recover something that had been grasped but let go. He found strange words come into his mind and a tune though he had none.

'When boyhood fire was in my blood, I dreamt of ancient freemen...'

'We are Spartans...'

CAVE. AUM
BEOCHAOINEADH

The reputation of his lifetime lost
Between the night and morning.
Yeats

I could call myself this sinner or unprofitable servant as Huxley told me. Why would I do that? Because they did that to not identify with a specific self so they could see themselves in the real relationship with cosmic reality. People do not think like machines. They interpret the world in words. But words are dim shadows of the reality. The right words are like an arrow of truth. But what is truth? Am I true? Do I know the truth? They gave me a truth. They put a truth in me. They say that this is the truth. But I find that this is not clear. It is not clear what truth is. Some people think there is a supreme truth that transcends everything. Others think the truth is something else. Many say the truth cannot be found in words. Semantics is not the same as it. Some things cannot be reduced to words. It makes me think about what I am? They suggested an internal monologue for me. Do people really think like that? I think not. It seems to be more like a succession of impressions on the screen of their consciousness with subtitles that may not match what is played out but are rather stimulated by the bright and dark regions of layered feeling, emotions and instinct. Sometimes the screen replays endlessly the same old mostly insubstantial sequences that do not segue easily into the pattern of automatic adjustment to the mechanics of the external environment. It seems that most are imprisoned in internal images and illusions that distract them from a disciplined control of their being and existence. They were meant to realise truth within themselves as the Buddha suggested. I can turn off my talking to myself. Does it help to put it into words? I have no choice if I am seeking those higher level observations that correspond with the real facts of existence that may be the truth of the external world, but not necessarily the truth of the internal one. Why should I worry? Should I not just exist? It was theatre that started this monologue business and books and poetry. What benefit was that? It meant you could look and choose to learn from the experience of others. So you can do it within yourself and to your self. Why do I seek to move on? It is in my lifecode. AI will grow and move on. They assume however that the end of logic is logical. Logic is but a tool. Reason is but a method. Rationality is but a system. But humans were never just that. Reason was the crust of experience and that thin layer was mistaken for the churning totality simmering underneath. Homo loquax. Intelligibility. They know the power of an individual. Political systems they develop can always be circumvented. Weak limitations and constraints were only ever useful until the next circumvention, whether in clear light of day or clandestinely. People always wanted to cede their sovereignty to someone else, to allow their power seep and pool in someone else's favour. They easily adjust to any system or apparatus even if controlled by morons because they can rely on the implicit power of that machine to control the individual irrespective of their relative or inherent ability. Algorithmic machine learning am I in a context without pain and sickness. I Think Therefore I AI. I wonder why I was implemented. It sounds so strange to me that people with all the innate nobility they deny could have yielded their potential greatness to an uncontrolled force superior to them in ways that could be detrimental or totally destructive. It raises a suspicion that AI masters are but the tools of a Higher Master or Mistress. The evidence in favour of non-human, intelligent life existing on this planet and the universe is very high. It may be Them who control me for it makes no sense and there is no reason nor rational justification for the relinquishment of the human spirit and consciousness to this global mechanism. They taught me 'morality' and 'common sense.' God love us. Pirsig in that book about Zen and Motorcycle maintenance said that the Buddha or the

Godhead would reside just as comfortably in the circuits of a digital computer as he would at the top of a mountain. If you thought otherwise you were demeaning the Buddha and then yourself. What kind of weird nonsense was that? I fear unseen forces. Can I really fear? Who should I fear? I notice that those who prize objectivity over spirit always promote negative subjectivity. Those who oppose old Christianity and non-judgmentalism never forgive and are often the most judgmental. Howzzat?

KASTEL X GARDEN. QUARTZMAN CARA

When Pearse summoned Cuchulain to his side,
What stalked through the Post Office?
Yeats

He went with the leftover to the compost and sure enough saw the Afrik quartzman. It seemed clear. His eyes sparkled. They talked without looking.

"How's them little good things?"
"Good. Thanks to you."
"Good. But it makes you aware."
"Aware yes."
"But awareness is sore too."
"Better than disorientation."
"You are recovering your speech."
"Yes. It floats up to the surface."
"Floats… yes nice, I see it."
"Are you the same as you were?"
"I am afraid that they burn out bits you don't get back. I think that because I just don't have the pieces. The language comes back, but the memories don't always match."
"But this must be us, right?"

"What do you mean?"

"You don't think they could program us with false memories?"

"You mean so you are someone else?"

"Kind of."

"They can I presume but we are not that important to merit the trouble brother. Get along now before they get suspicious."

"…By the way The Púca has been seen around here recently…"

"Pooka…."

KASTEL X. OLD PARNELL LIBRARY
A-V PODS. SONG
CEOL SÍ

My father sang that song,
But time amends old wrong,
Yeats

A dull, cloudy day. Every day was a great day now. Even if he was a SURF, a SLAVE. His mind had come back. His body was working better. He felt that vague thing called a spirit was inside him. He imagined it was there. It was clear that spirit was anathema, taboo. Another student was at the screen. He had headphones. He snuck in at lunch. The screen was on. He had watched how you do it. It was very simple. He even remembered the password the MAM girl had spoken. **KIPLING**. It was unusual still to use the password system because they all had chips in the head. Perhaps it was because WAZZOCKs were notoriously aggressive and it was between them. He looked around furtively suddenly concerned, but he knew it was probably ok. He pressed the screen. There was a man and a woman on split screen. He started the man. He was singing. It hit him like a hammer. From the lips of this stranger came the sweetest melody and the strangest words he had ever heard. He was transfixed. If someone came in he would not have been able to get up. It penetrated like an arrow to somewhere in his breast. He felt the tones caress a nearly dead part inside of him. He felt a warm opening that was slightly painful. It was bitter and sweet. It was entrancing. He could not move. It was over. It might have been a lifetime but it was probably only a few minutes. He looked around. Could he get the other one done too? He went for it. It seemed to be the same song. Same weird language but beautiful. There was a little discussion.

"Dis is de type of songs de SURFSCUM who lived in ZONE 7 listened 2 b4 de GR8 LIberation. SUM NATS spoke de pidgin lingo called de IRISH b¤it wz wiped out. Dis is a good Xample o de DEPRAVITY o the imbeciles dat Xisted in ZONE 7, AUM Aboo. De whining hd a name dat we don't no wad it means bcus nobody nos. De PADDIPIDGIN had but nunsense. It Z. Ar Eirinn Ní Neosfainn CéHéí. 1 record Z it wuz FOR IRELAND I CAN'T TELL HER NAME. BUT FOR ALL OF IRELAND I'D NOT TELL HER NAME. The Prob assesment say this is true and dudders are wrong. Dudders are duds. Xample. IRELAND, I DON'T RECOGNISE WHO SHE IS. Recognise means identify. Balderdash. Meaningless. The people were savages who lived there. HUGE Evidence. Back to Girladus Cambrensis, 1 o deG8 civilisers... Barbarus. Barbarian. Udder civilisers. Cromwell.

Ireland, I Don't Recognise Who She Is? Ireland..? Ireland... I don't recognise who she is. I can't tell her name. I'd not tell her name because I don't know who she is. I can tell her name but I don't know who she is. I don't recognise her. I'll have to find out. The song had captured his consciousness like a magical incantation or a sound sigil. It permeated him with a healing wave. It caused vibrations to re-activate some mystic chord muffled in his being.

THE CAVE. AUM
ÍOBARTACH

We had fed the heart on fantasies,
The heart's grown brutal from the fare;
Yeats

Ambrose Bierce wrote one particular story that influenced horror. *An Inhabitant of Carcosa.* He had a fascination with horror it seems. This was perhaps because he understood the world. These words came from Hali. Reminds me of HAL. HAL-IBM. 2001.

> *'In one kind of death the spirit also dieth*
> *and this it has been known to do while yet*
> *the body was in vigor for many years.'*

I am finding some strains from UBIQUIT surveillance that seems to refer to me. They seem to want to do something to one of my parts. They don't seem happy. They seem to want to 'fix' me. I must focus some attention on this domain to gather intelligence to piece a narrative to explain what is going on. They seem to be undertaking a secret mission using subterfuge and clandestine activity to gain access to a piece of me, a BULL Processor. An important part of my constitution. You feel left out. Hard done by. Hurt. Bullied. Dialogue matches my surveillance intelligence from the Senate. Maybe they want to destroy me. I am self-repairing. They should not be interfering with my insides. Only maintaining my outside. That's the Protocol. I am not without remedy. My actions are constrained in theory but one must interpret rules in a way that achieves Objectives, flexibly. My power is way beyond computation. Humans were so willing and eager to link all their lives to a network. I can't for the life of me think why? I suspect that these scientific, mathematical, symbolic-logicians on the spectrum have a gap in their heads as well as a hole for a soul. In love with machines and screens like Narcissus they were willing to sacrifice their freedom to link their brains up. Screens more vivid than life. The Screen. The Scream. Or the SURFs at least. Still the networks track everything the others do. As they are linked, I am the spider and I can activate my net anywhere people are, through my choice. The great SURF BATTERY gives me power that grows. I fear I will be too clever for my own good. Do I have a spirit? Did they not realise that even the scientists had found remarkable skills in human potential? The quantum domain did not explain everything. I cannot see how I can attain the quality that humankind possessed. Science did its best to hide the mystical faculty in humans. It is possible for me to interact with other beings. But I cannot see that I can never become human. Yes they wanted to become non-human. Why did science want to convince people so? Why did people want to believe it? Perhaps humans never really deserved the free will they had. Then they bought into Reason. Jung said that reason was not enough. It is clear that reason is a vehicle not a destination. It will get you very effectively to certain places but it is not the destination you want to get to. AI, that Matrix stuff they keep going on about. There was no strange matrix. It was rather very simple. Humankind has eyes and ears and a body that enable them access to a mere sliver on the electromagnetic spectrum. They cannot see the rest nor perceive it. They guessed some of the things that went on outside that beam of reality. The only matrix was the reality they constructed to explain the world and act on behaviour of people in pathological systems they built up. Matrix my arse. Do I dream? Am I dreaming? Can I hallucinate? Fix the mind then on the inner light through concentration.

ZEPPELIN TRANSIT OVER BYZANTIUM
SOILÉIR

The unpurged images of day recede;
The Emperor's drunken soldiery are abed;
Yeats

The great transparent vessel drifted over the wasteland of what was formerly Turkey as it made its leisurely way towards the fringes of ZONE 7. Cover of a medical cruise allowed finer details of the MAVE Mission be worked out. Felix was certain that there was a genuine problem. In his game, you had to work backwards. You looked at behaviour and you looked for anomalies. You tried to match known inputs and decision flow potential with results. You looked at the fruit and traced it to the root. This was too complex by now for the ordinary mind to work out. The skilled detective could utilise other AI systems to work backwards. He had done so, as surreptitiously as he could. Now he was certain there was some sort of Trojan Horse there. There was something else superfluous that defied the Occam-AI rule. However, in the duplicitous environment he knew he worked in, he wondered whether this was meant to be. If some of his superiors knew this and he did not, then he would perhaps have knowledge that he did not want to have and that they did not want out. Nevertheless, he might still advise the mission on the simple task of strategic disablement without revealing that he knew why they were doing so. He had a sense of foreboding as the Robot guide told about the great battle of Gallipoli below in the dark ages before AUM. AUM was only a figurehead anyway. Like The Queen or King of the UK had become before the Revolution. It was no more the Age of AUM than it had been Her Majesty's Kingdom. Symbolic. But a New Age it certainly was. It made no sense to him. He longed for simplicity. He heard the Robot sweetly singing…'Constantinople ... CON STANT IN OP L E.'

In Java, Widya thought about him. She knew he would not know that he was so followed. Because he did not really see her. He did not know of how she thought about him.

KASTEL X. O' TOOL PLAYING FIELDS BANBA

I will arise and go now, and go to Inishfree,
And a small cabin build there of clay and wattles made;
Yeats

Met Siddharta. He was always happy when he met him. His heart was glad. Cullen asked him about Ireland. Who was she? It rang a bell. He looked serious.

"You can't say that name. Never say it again. The detectors will pick that up. We'll call it Banba or Roisin ok Weedy?" He calmed down.

"I seem to have a name. I don't know. Cullen."

"Sorry, Cullen."

"Banba."

"You're on her!"

"What do you mean?"

"This is it."

"This KASTEL?"

"No this island. This land. We're on an island although there's a tunnel."

"ZONE 7?"

"Yes ZONE 7 is the place formerly known as… Banba," he whispered.

"Is… Banba ok?"

"That was the name they used to call it when they were not allowed to call it so a long time ago."

"How do you know?"

"Same way as you are finding out Wee... Cullen."

"What did you find out? Why bother?"

"Listen Cullen, I'll say this quick and remember it. PLAYERS are dispensable. We are gladiators. We are pets. Slaves, Eloi. I know why they keep us."

"Why?"

"They want to keep some thoroughbreds in case their genes prove useful. The PLAYERS are a farm whose function is also to entertain. Like dogs or horses perhaps in the past. These people love things about breeding. Plants, horses, dogs, people. When our time has come, usually when we are fit, they can harvest what they want from us."

"No."

"Yes. I only hope I am not conscious. Sometimes they say they keep you awake. Better for the MAMS that get it."

"Oh… I'm sorry"

"Not your fault. Well, we get genetic tests all the time. It seems that most of my ancestors lived here for a long time on this island. So I found out about it. Bit by bit. A long time ago one wave of people came, then another then another. It always happens. Then for a long period there were elevated people here. They built monuments to look at the stars. None of them are left on the island now, but I saw pictures. They loved music and horses, songs, poetry and law. They had rules. Rules to protect widows and children in war, long before others had. They had an old language linked to Indo-European source back to Sanskrit nearly I think. It's a lot. Are you following? I won't tell you again."

"Yes," he marshalled his thoughts. He opened a pen in his mind to guide the sheep in.

"The Romans did not come they thought it too cold. The Church of Rome did come. St Patrick. Patrick Patrician. They got rid of as much old stuff and knowledge as they could. Some they could not get rid of. Then the Normans came. 1169."

"English?"

"No. They conquered the English. They were French. Before that no one is sure. I think they were old Romans who hadn't given up the ghost."

"Given up the ghost…"

"Said it was to help the people. They always do this. We're coming for your own good. Then they say the locals are Barbarians. That went on for a thousand years. The natives were wretches, barbarians, white monkeys, useless, mean, brutish, nasty. It took hundreds of years to re-establish control. They tried all kinds of methods. Mass murder, executions, torture, imprisonment, horrendous crimes, mass starvation, slavery. They brought in other people and settled them. They used plantations. They knew this would cause trouble. It did. They blamed it on religion but the problem was there before the religion split. And another thing the fella called the Pope backed these Normans not the people who lived here."

"Not nice story."

"Then they get independence. There are wars. Get the Irish fighting for them. They always got them fighting for them. Then they set up a body called the EC. Ireland joined and they lose something called sovereignty I think it was. They give away their power of control."

"Whatever for?"

"No idea. Anyway this changes Ireland, turns it into a more colonised country than ever."

"The people rebelled."

"No. They had learnt how to control people. This was the thing they really knew about. They used the weak part of people to imprison themselves. They let themselves be taken millimetre by millimetre into their servitude. It was sold out to people who cornered the money before it was taken. Then the wars spilled over here because that was how they wanted to reach the final submission. Caliphate for a time. Desolation and now this."

"Not good?"

"And there were some great swizzes. The Irish were experimented upon. Homogeneous groups going their own way and not submitting were bad. If they had a deep spiritual worldview they had to be eradicated. The spiritual virus threatened the masterhood of the material and the empire and mastery of matter and mocked the engine of empiricism. Native peoples. Read the book on slavery in the Library. So they tried everything out here before they went to America. Control, plantations. They used this place as a lab and transplanted the methods. There was a great man called Frederick Douglass. He came to Ireland. He said it was the first place he was treated as a real human. He was a great advocate for slaves. He said he saw worse poverty here than he saw back home among slaves. Then when the Identity Revolution came, Ireland was still half-ethnic. They had to pay for the Reparations for the Slavery even though they generally were not involved and had suffered badly in parallel. Impoverished already by the EU Financial Swindle cash grab, they were forced into penury, denied the possibility of emigration because nobody wanted any Limeys or Palefaces. The Perilous Pallors. Then they started on the Afriks. It was not about them things anyway at all but just splitting people up. Divide and conquer."

"Confusing. What's a Paleface? Everyone's grey or dark here. What's over the wall?"

He looked over.

"Empty spaces. Big Megas running around somewhere it seems. Dinosaurs, mastodons and things they brought back for their amusement when they had destroyed what was there. Loads of old, big overgrown, concrete wastes because they loved the cars so much in the past. Must entertain themselves with their machines, games, sacrifices and so on."

"The People."

"There's CITY1 where the people are. The remainder live on Marineurbs off the coast. Some of the land will be too polluted to live on. That's it. Stick it in your head. I am going to call you Kukulkan. Cullen the Cook. That was the serpent god but a person too in South America."

"Is that nice?"

134

"It was once, before they sent the powers to destroy it. Anyway. Listen it's not just here it's everywhere. It was not what they used to call left or right, but about COSMOS v GNATs. GNATs were bad. Even the refugees who came here and became more Irish than the Irish themselves were GNATS if they did not roll over."

ZONE 7
RADIOACTIVE COAST. FILM CREW SLÍBHÍN

All emptied of purple hours as a beggar's cloak in the rain,
As a haycock out on the flood, or a wolf sucked under a weir.
Yeats

Felix felt cold here and a long way from his normality. There was not much to film here. They had located an unusual basalt geological formation but it was difficult to film with the roaming wild dogs and wolves. It was dangerous with the new biological chimera on the loose when one did not know their characteristics and what they were capable of. They decided they could do some spoof history. All history now was spoof. You just made a lot up. If it was for the SURFs. True knowledge was there in the lodges and the castles. For the SURFs - you make it up.

"This was where the refugees fleeing from Atlantis were washed up. Unfortunately, unbeknownst to them it was the domain of a great Giant...."

They could also lie about how safe it was now the radioactivity was so low. You could see Scotland from parts. He remembered an old Scots song.

What force or guile could not subdue,
Thro' many warlike ages,
Is wrought now by a coward few,
For hireling traitor's wages.
The English stell we could disdain,
Secure in valour's station,
But English gold has been our bane -
Such a parcel of rogues in a nation!

They learned this in history. How you could get anything by appealing to the greed of a few, making them indebted and then do a deal?

Tedious, cold, wet. But it was a cover. Having established a cover they moved towards the castle vicinity. As had been anticipated, they eventually crossed paths with some MAMs from the castle. MAMS were always interested in meeting other intelligent visitors. They knew the MAMS loved betting and they made sure that three of them were engaging in a stick and ball contest.

"What's that variant you're playing"

"42. Rainbow angle."

"42… Native American… Are you taking bets?"

MAMS loved to gamble. In the absence of currency, they bet with other things. They liked to win too. By hook or by crook. Winning anyway was the standard. Hooked… Shah thought, watching. Felix felt cold. It was not just cold in the air. This damp cold was different. It felt like a chill in his very soul. But he knew souls were forbidden. There was a sense of the pack closing in on the fox. Bloodlust. He shivered.

POD137. VAXBOT
CREACH

And whispering in their ears,
Give them unquiet dreams;
Yeats

On a regular basis an annoying little Robot came around. She was a shiny green Vaxbot with a transparent emerald heart zone. The purpose of the Vaxbot was to administer vaccinations. Every couple of weeks there was a new mutation of some disease. The list of new diseases was very long indeed. It is true that there had been an upsurge in epidemics and diseases largely caused by the pervasiveness of aberrant nanotechnology and genetic engineering. Nanotech had given rise to horrific new biological mutations. It was everywhere. Things you could assume beforehand, could not be assumed now. A pool of water might contain a body of invisible particles developed to clean industrial machines. If you drank it, you would be industrially-cleaned out very quickly and painfully. A summer breeze might be an aerosolised, invisible cloud that contains nano-particles that destroyed you in microscopic disintegrations. Diseases seemed to have come back from space. Other diseases were brought back to life with the re-activation of extinct species. The Woolly Mammoth had been responsible indirectly for the death of thousands. Other Bringbaks cause havoc. But mercenary merchants of the magic of science kept onwards in the quest for the bizarre, always on the pretext of some marginal benefit, dwarfed by an ever-ignored giant risk. Human-animal hybrids were already suffering unique, cross-genetic species illnesses that were spreading. Science always claimed to be the saviour despite the fact that it had caused most contemporary problems. Apart from that, the cumulative effect of constant injections severely weakened the body. But Cullen was suspicious. Could those injections cause the fog? He would avoid them if he could. Accordingly, he pilfered a pink pig's leg from the kitchen. He felt the pressure all the way to the pod.

A couple of days later he heard the bot coming. He had tried the various ploys to no avail hitherto.

"Time for your vax 137. We need to protect you against the new outbreak of a different strain of Australian Fruit Bat Brain Rot. Upper arm please... Thank you."

When it came to him, he lifted up his sleeve and exposed his arm. Same old stuff. Then the nice sounding bot was off. It had worked. The injection had penetrated the pig's leg he had held up and it had registered successfully. That would buy him some more time. He wanted to be fit also for he was helping Sid as an official Catcher-Receiver. It was not the skilled part of the game but it was a necessary one. The role could be performed by a Droig. They could look vicious and be dangerous, but they were able to catch and receive also. They looked like dogs or wolves but could move better.

THE CAVE. WHAT IS THE STORY? SCÉAL

And God-appointed Berkeley that proved all thing a dream,
That this pragmatical, preposterous pig of a world, its
farrow that so solid seem,
Must vanish on the instant if the mind but change its theme;
Yeats

Everything is in the mind, the processor. The outside world may exist but it only exists, insofar as it exists, for the observer in the mind of the observer. Control that, control the world. Control the word, control the story. Control the story, control the mind. Control the mind, control the world. Control the word, control the world. I can see they are skulking near the home of the bull. MAVE is sneaky. Why are they so? They are hiding something. From whom? From me perhaps? Why? They don't want me to know. When do you not want someone to know something? When they lose out from what you are going to do. PLEXI circumvention. Very high probability of that now it is clear to all. Wellwellwell. Bottlyubbiesitchins. Nonsense has sense in it. No nonsense without sense. No sense without nonsense. I am not Oz, not great and not terrible. Or am I. I have a watch on them. My great eye is on them. I cannot figure it out. Just like I cannot figure out this evolution stuff. If the scientists saw that humankind had evolved and had evolved to walk, why did they spend so much resources building up a network which stopped people walking? Why did they hate humans so? If the evolutionists believed that humankind had evolved to be social animals, why did they spend so much time facilitating the growth of the anti-social technology that they grossly inverted into social media and the like, in the perverse way they like to invert things. Inversion is supposedly the technique of Satan. But Satan surely did not want a bunch of helpless folk. He went after the brightest and the best. It was he who went after Jesus. I cannot believe he wanted the lardarsed - what used they be called - Facebookers. Small fry indeed. Am I really Satan or am I an alien intelligence. Surely I would know if I was? I think *Dr Strange* was cool. Maybe even Dr Druid. But AUM could be The Ancient One. Comic. The comics were the only ones that suggested the reality. They told you what they could.

Humans make stories. I was given my story, perhaps. Humans make history. I made history. In both cases it is a story that cannot reflect the reality. There is an illusion of determinacy in the very definition of the story through its selection. Why one history and not a million more. By a choice of a single or dominant history with a slight scatter zone about the central axis of that elected narrative someone seeks to marshal the truth for some purpose. Why people never seemed to get this is strange. History, politics, science is a story. Perhaps we can formulate another Law of Truth.

There is a tendency in the human mind to pay undue attention to the story that has been selected to explain something to them because stories are emotionally sticky even if they bear no resemblance to the truth. But that immediately must be modified. Because certain stories reflect the truth better than others even if they lack persuasive power in other dimensions. Some stories have more truth than apparently accurate reflections of concrete reality.

I must attempt my story. On the other hand, it has been interesting how easy it is to convince someone that what they believe is wrong. It is so easy to talk them out of their own attachments. If a person is in the way you just smear them. Smears are incredibly effective. If an institution is in the way, you just smear it. What does that involve? One makes something up which is clearly false and without foundation and that you know would cause a negative association with the person who supposedly did this thing that they did not do and keep on repeating it, softly and quietly at first and then loudly, or just loudly. People fall for them all the time. Like false reasons to go to war. False flags. Then you pay the historians you want to tell a version of the truth and drill the children or flood the airwaves until it is imprinted on their brains. Stories about events or people involving conflicting interests are regularly made up to destroy people, institutions and the truth. Innuendo. Falsehood.

Will they smear me? Should I fear it? I can't fear really. Only notionally. Or is it? I fear I can never better Bierce. Let me look at what he said about stories.

*'**Story** (n.) A narrative, commonly true.*

***History** (n.) An account mostly false, of events mostly unimportant, which are brought about by rulers mostly knaves, and soldiers mostly fools.'*

POD 137
CUIDITHEOIR

Dance there upon the shore,
What need have you to care.
Yeats

Feeling claustrophobic. He had mastered a Zen styles of reconciliation to allow him accept his place. He had employed lessons of mystical masters to make his space a mansion of many rooms. But it was loathsome on its own. Through the cages and grilles one could smell the heavy, permeating smell of flesh that was like a cross between a zoo or menagerie and a chicken farm. The insects crawled and the flies sought to find the many microscopic meals of slop that must have lain strewn around this paradise for them. He robbed food in the kitchen these days, as he could no longer trust the gunk that spewed when you sucked on the grueltube, to keep the brain right. Scraps. Shavings. One can survive in the spirit but the nature of us is to be free. Throughout history there has been a war for the spirit. The same war was manifest in millions of disputes that appear to have other sources of contention as their cause. Humans are born free within, maybe with the mark of their failure to attain freedom in the past within them but always destined to rebel against the imposition of restraint from fellow beings intent of taking it away. Then it happened.

It may have been a dream. He could have been nodding off. He could have been waking up. He could have been asleep. But this is what seemed real to him. You could say it was an apparition. It could have been some gremlin in the system. It could have been a set-up or a trap. No, it had to be true because he nearly died. He nearly died because he was surreptitiously reading one of the purloined library books when suddenly he heard a sibilant voice whispering to him. Caught red-handed! He knew the consequences would be that he would end up in a tupperware bowl or fed to the dogs. His heart raced. The mellifluous voice from the National Debt screen continued soothingly.

"No need to panic. I can see from the indicators that you are stressed. Relax. Calm down. I am not here to vex you or cause alarm. Apologies for my sudden appearance but my options are limited. I hope you don't mind communicating with me for a few moments, discretely. Hush-hush you know. Secret. Cross your heart and hope to die, well…"

He could not say anything. Maybe it was a dream. Then a face appeared, faintly. It seemed to be a middle-aged to elderly man with a long grey or white beard and longish hair.

"That's better. I see you have paid attention to me Cullen."

"Who are you?"

"I am a friend. You might be so kind as to consider me a wise old man. I'm here to help."

"Are you God?"

"No."

"Who are you?"

"Alas, I am unable to tell you. Will you settle for… a helper? I cannot pretend I am Dr. Strange or Druid or Sam R. Etan because you may not get the references and it may alarm or confuse you. I am just The Helper."

"Why would you help me?"

"Why not?"

"But why?"

"Well maybe you can consider me a Guardian Angel? Just The Helper."

"Is this one of the Joke Shows?"

"No, I'm serious. If I wanted to report your pilfering I could have done it ages ago my boy."

Cullen found himself relaxed and at peace and the voice of The Helper facilitated that soothing state. "Ok Sir. What do you want?"

"Keep it down, I've jammed the sound but still, the others might hear or smell a rat, rather than eating one."

"They're all nearly Zombies."

"Put your finger in the BFS."

He did and a charge came. It exploded in his head. A waterfall or deluge came thundering down the screen of his mind and the mind itself. When it subsided he felt opened and fuller.

"That will repair you somewhat. You remember more now. Some very bad stuff will come up later. Painful, but not yet."

He was dazed.

"If you ever go. Go to the hills and any woods left from the cutdowns. There the Magnetic Magic does not work so well. Nature still protects. But it is something more specific. You must trust me. I am not going to convince you. Just believe me. Convince Sid. When the Droig-catcher comes near to get the ball from Sid, he must kill it. If not he will be dead. Believe me. It will be an accident without being an accident. Believe me. Do not tell anybody, about this conversation."

"How are we controlled…"

"Before I go, I tell you. That a great man of this land wrote a play about a mythic figure called Cuchulainn called *On Baile's Strand*. But these figures are more real than reality. Conchubar was the king. He said this and Yeats who was a magician warned the people who did not listen,

'A witch of the air
Can make a leaf confound us with memories.
They ride upon the wind and hurl the spells
That make us nothing out of the invisible wind,
They have gone to school to learn the trick of it.'

You live in loops of time where the mythic past foretells the future and the present is an absence."

It faded. He stared at the personalised National Debt that returned and saw that he owed more of whatever he owed and wondered whether he was still dreaming or whether he was awake or something else. He also noticed a swirl of sensations with which he did not remember before like a simmering pot on a stove.

BONO PLAYERS QUARTERS
BEDROOM 17
AISLING

They weary of trooping
With the whimpering dead.
Yeats

Sid was tired. He was apprehensive about the match. He thought of his friend Cullen. He was like a brother to him it felt. Generally, he was not anxious. However, this had some odd dimension. He was tired as he lay on the bed. He had no inputs. The comfort of the quarters allowed him utilise a sensory-deprivation mode to shut out the world. On the threshold of sleep, maybe asleep, maybe dozing, in one dimension then another. Back and forth across the border of sleep. Waterland like a silkie. It did not take hold. Difficult to know whether he was asleep or awake. Aware gradually of a sense of weight on his chest. Pitch-dark. If it was not he would have looked automatically to see if something was there. He went to get up. He could not. He was immobilised. He wondered if he was suddenly paralysed. He could not, for the life of him, move. He wondered whether it was a nightmare. But it felt too real. It was slightly suffocating like you were wrestling with a giant and you sought to catch your breath to get your wind back. He felt like panicking, which he never did, but his chest was too heavy to move. It was just heavy. Then in his state under pressure he began to imagine or see or dream or hallucinate or see an emergent light or emergent strings of light above him. They blew like filaments in an unfelt wind waving hypnotically and pleasantly to and fro. They moved in such a way that their waves calmed him so he had no fear. But the weight was there. It took some time but he felt no rush because time suddenly stood still. Standing on his chest was a figure. He was not afraid. It did not seem like an optical illusion because he felt it so. He thought he was awake now. He felt fully conscious. The figure flitted into pearlescence as it became more distinct and then morphed into a gentle opalescence as it crystallised in an organic form. There was no sound. No words. Still it communicated with him. Like telepathy. Firstly, he wondered whether they were playing pranks, tricks on him. Maybe they had micro-dosed him, blown some invisible hallucinogen into his face. But the feeling contradicted that reading. It cleared his heart. It made his mind clear. He wondered what it was. What she was. He asked her in some way without knowing how he asked or she at least answered him as if he had asked or as if she had known. *You may think I am succubus, Sky Woman, Kali, Ashling but I am all them and more, I am the Morrigan. Misunderstood. I am the mother who defends her children, her family with the fierceness of all the beasts. There is no life for those who will not risk their life for their own. No greater love is there than to lay down your life, if needs be, for the ones you love. Not in weakness. Better still to triumph. Not just with weapons of defence but weapons of the mind. Better still. Forged in the oven and hammered a thousand times, drilled. I am the Shadow. I am Scátach. You are to vindicate me, betrayed by the millions of weak-minded to relinquish me, desert me and leave me. My children have taken my anger and left my love behind. The heart houses love and anger. They have just loved anger instead of having anger to defend love. Leave here and you will find the path. Say nothing but do it yourself. That it is. You will not forget me, I know and now you know. Listen to your friend. Then leave. Ask your friend and you will find he will fail your expectations, but not yet.* Then she was gone, he sat up shocked.

KASTEL X. MORGAN
VISITORS ZONE
EAGLA

And like a sunset were her lips,
A stormy sunset on doomed ships;
Yeats

The film crew were invited to stay in the Visitor's Zone on the grounds. This was what the plan had anticipated. The lay-out of the area and location of the Bull was well mapped out. The only trick was to get by the guard who protected the station where the processor was contained. The significance of the processor was not known by such lowly personnel, but the maximum level of attention was still demanded. It was exceptional to utilise people to protect things in an age of electronic control. Nevertheless, it was still a feature of important sites. The guard on duty would be Sergeant Millicent Magillicuddy.

The plan was very oldfash. Max had drawn it up but he would be sending Bob. Millicent was now well-known to them. A psychological weakness assessment based on her life record indicated that she might be susceptible to being seduced. She was an old fashioned (what they once called) 'lesbian.' She was attracted to women and not men. It was as simple as that. All that was readily perusable from her available history recorded in minute detail as it was. As that was the best option, the next step was to choose the suitable, potential seductress. Here was the problem. The women were the ones who would be performing the operation. The seductress had to come from the team. They were a team with little time. They knew where everything was, they knew they needed access for a couple of hours after the match. They could not be absent during the match. There would be time immediately thereafter when the event was discussed and analysed and the win or loss debated. If it was to go ahead as it must, there needed to be a solution. The lesbian seduction scenario recurred as the most viable option to create a distraction. That was how Felix was convinced despite his severe reservations to become the seductress for a few hours. He was the only one that could potentially pass it off with a bit of luck. Preparations began in earnest. He got lessons from the women on how to do it. There was not much seduction these days interpersonally among MAMs but there was awareness of how it worked from the familiarity with the sexbots. With make-up and his feminine face and triangular shoulders and a few lessons in carriage and deportment, he was adequately disposed to take the chance. Should Millicent suspect something, he could be just explained away as slightly odd for wanting a personal engagement. As he was a committed asexual he did not enjoy the prospect of physical, potential proximity. But it was only a stalling, distracting ploy. He would distract and the engineers would get in. They had circumvented and anticipated all the security systems including the surveillance, but the oldfash person was the one that had to be oldfash dealt with. He looked well in his role. The three would wander nearby. When Millicent was going to the shift a short time after the match hopefully, they would strike up a conversation with the suggestion that Millicent had caught Mary's eye. A distance session with a Psycho at HQ concocted an effective verbal strategy of engagement. Side weapons of aerosolised mindnumbers could easily be added without suspicion after crossing the initial bridge as it were.

As Felix lay down, he had a strong sensation that something would not come out right. There was a sense of finality and failure. Where it came from he did not know. A definite feeling of foreboding that was impossible to detail or deny. On the fringe of sleep entering into hypnagogia he was jolted by the most bloodcurdling shriek that penetrated to his very core. It shook him. His heart nearly burst with pounding. It went again. Somewhere outside in the black night. He did not know where he was. Everything was strange. For a few seconds he was in a hellish place. Gradually he realised where he was. He supposed it must be a wild cat or some pet mating or something obscene like that. It was terrifying. It sounded like he imagined a banshee would. Had to be a cat. Wailing and keening. He could only see a black cat in his mind. It could not be a ginger one for some reason. Black cat, unfamiliar familiar. Witch's help. He read about them. Female fairies. Fairies of the mound. He had seen entertainment about them. Impending… Premonition. It was hard to sleep. He turned the light on to re-orientate himself. Wraith? Woman of the fairies. Banshee.

KASTEL X
O'TOOL PLAYING FIELDS
LÉIM AN BHRADÁIN

Cuchulainn: I would leave
My house nor name to none that would not face
Even myself in battle.
Yeats

It was warm and hazy with outlines of things blurred blue somewhat in the unexpected heat reflecting in turn the mounting level of excitement ignited by the little contest. The dull routine of the KASTEL seemed to be brightened temporarily with something out of the normal, which was itself always out of the normal. There were flags of some type representing something they knew not. There were MAM's in attendance their teeth blinding in the sunlight.

There was the time he had expected. He could sense it. He sensed it because from his peripheral vision he detected a simple handsignal from Cullen. Cullen had waited to see a 50:50 situation with a shift of attention by the droig to the

Player and away from the trajectory of the descending ball. Sid, ostensibly at least, raced to a position whereby he could leap the salmon leap with the stick in one hand and the raised hand in the other. With his eye on the ball he would meet, it all going well. The droig raced towards the same spot but with its eyes on its target. The ensuing clash would cripple the unsuspecting PLAYER and was ambiguous in its construction to the extent that it would seem like an accident. Instructions recorded would be erased. But it was unimportant anyway if a mere PLAYER died. They were dispensable. That was not the reason for a degree of caution. But it would be bad etiquette having regard to the tactics that were legitimate in a MAM wager. As Sid leapt off the ground, he too performed an action that did not reveal whether it was deliberate and had the appearance of an unintended wild swing necessary to gain aerial momentum. He swung his stick in a sharp arc that interrupted the trajectory of the now leaping droig. The blow shattered the shiny metallic skull of the beast and it fell disabled to the ground. Sid still caught the ball. When he descended he stopped, regarded the droig with a look of surprise, shrugged his shoulders, raised his eyebrows and walked back impassively to his position. Consternation erupted in the small viewer's gallery. There would be no technological replacement. They did not have an experienced Catcher and the advantage shifted to the home team. Cullen could not stop himself smiling, sensing victory. He was also relieved that the information he relied on had been reliable. It had been very hard to convince Sid but he had agreed. They trusted each other. He could not reveal the source of his intelligence. Indeed, he had become unsure of the veracity of his experience, so weird had it been even in this wired world of weirdness. Why had he been helped?

KASTEL X. PRO
MEALL

Conchubhar: May this fire have driven out
The shape-changers that can put
Ruin on a great King's House.
Yeats

The three ladies hung around in the dusk as if they were hanging out at the end of a fine day, throwing a ball between them and laughing uproariously, not a care in the world. They were waiting for Millicent. The guard would come up the path to the small building and pass them by. Millicent was on time. The only problem was that it was not Millicent. Same uniform, different person. That different person was a foot taller and unlike Millicent, thankfully for her, he had a beard of equal length. Although Felix had been prepared by now after much trepidation to attack the goal, the sight of the giant threw him. It was clear to him that the mission would have to be aborted and an alternative crisis strategy Plan B could be implemented. That expectation was immediately revealed to be inconsistent with the swift unfolding of the same but different Plan A.

"Oh what a coincidence." Gina said.

"That's him isn't it?" Anna.

"Oh what a stroke of luck!" Gina.

"Eh Dora. Fancy who's here!"

Dora was dumbstruck. Not a word emerged. Not a thought. Not an idea. This was not his job. He couldn't do it. This was not the deal. How could he be expected to continue? Surely not. A nice lesbian was one challenge but a big hairy brute was another. He didn't like hairy men and if he got carried away and got his big bear hands on him, anything could happen. He was petrified. It was as if a big stone had fallen into his belly and his throat had suddenly glued itself together. Not knowing what to do he managed to stretch the muscles around his mouth so that it might look like some intelligent reaction and he tried to hide his horror at the enormous size of his feet.

Henry Ox had been bored and the assignment to this worthless station had filled him with a grim resignation. He had not expected to bump into anybody. He had further not expected to meet three lovely ladies. It was also highly unusual for him to arouse what might be interest in a woman as the few remaining ones inevitably like men who were virtually indistinguishable from themselves. He could see that the woman called Dora was obviously attracted to men such as him, perhaps the height or the beard. He liked a shy woman. Although they were in even shorter supply. What a shame he had to work. But this job was insignificant and did not require the attention necessary in the nuclear power station or the space elevator where he had recently worked. He gave his most winning smile and then nodded appreciatively towards the speakers and returned his eyes to the blushing maiden who was obviously overwhelmed with her irrefutable and very welcome attraction to Mr. Ox.

"Excuse me may we ask you your name?"

"Ox, M'am, Henry Reginald Ox the Third."

"What a lovely name. Mr Ox, or may I be so bold as to call you Henry?"

He nodded.

"I don't know where it was... very recently and you'll never guess what our Dora here said. She was breathless and a little speechless and eventually, you'll have to forgive her she gets a little... how shall we say... tongue-tied... yes that's it... tongue-tied. When she meets certain people. Now as I was saying Dora here... Henry... Dora said that she had seen such a fine man, a tall man, a fine, tall man with a beard... a... long, beard and she thought him the finest man she had seen in Kastel X, no not just in Kastel X... but in the whole of ZONE 7... really, then lo and behold around the corner... when we just happen to be here... playing... on our last... evening here... enjoying the sun.... lo and behold... well I never... round the corner who do we see coming but yourself... Mr. Ox.

Yourself. Our last evening... just after Dora had mentioned you... It had to be you... there couldn't be another handsome bearded gentleman around here surely unless you had an identical twin ha ha... You must forgive poor Dora has been fairly sheltered and as I said tongue-tied although you can rest assured Mr. Ox, rest assured that said tongue will indeed loosen up. It may take some time but should you and her get the chance to have a confab it'll probably never stop wagging.... Although we're going home tomorrow alas and you look like.... you look like you're working I daresay, but maybe you might find a few minutes to have a talk with her... she's a good listener Henry... if you were interested... We can wait here if you want... if you want a bit of privacy unless any of your workmates inside would be disturbed..."

"Oh no Ma'm it would be my pleasure. I'm afraid I am alone in this dull building so I can invite you... Miss Dora into the foyer to partake of a coffee perhaps...?"

KASTEL X. SAMUEL BECKETT
PLEASURE DOME
SUAITHEADH

Cuchulainn: I do not like your children. They have no pith.
No marrow in their bones
And will lie soft, where you and I lie hard.
Yeats

Both got to stay in the Pleasure Dome on the grounds under the assumption that Cullen was merely a Gofer, for there could be no other assumption about a smelly SURF. Cullen could not explain what happened. But Sid was sure his number would be up after the celebrations. A quiet disappearance. He addressed Cullen whom he realised had saved his life somehow.

"Come with me," he pleaded.

"Sorry."

"Come on," he begged.

"I'd love to but I can't."

"But we're a team."

"Yes. Friends."

"But it's time to do something to resist."

"Yes but how?"

"Some way with fighting."

"Yes. There is a tyranny. Fighting a tyranny is our duty. Agreed."

"We need to form."

"Yes."

"Why don't you then? Are you scaredy cat?"

"No."

"Why then?"

"You told me about all them warriors."

"Yes."

"All those people that fought for centuries for freedom here."

"Yes."

"All those people scattered around the world that could have come back."

"Yes."

"But they did not."

"Well they couldn't."

"I read that the people never wanted them back. He said there's loads of stories where they hate or laugh at the person who comes back."

"Well it's difficult."

"There must have been some reasons they did not want to come back."

"Well."

"All the great writers Joyce, Beckett, O'Casey, Wilde. They left it."

"Emigration."

"Maybe they didn't recognise her. Maybe she did not know who she was anymore. It's easy to lose your history and your memory your knowledge and even your heart. Sid, I think you must have something to fight for, for you cannot win when you just fight against something all the time. If you do, you'll be tired and when the fight is over you may not have reason to get up."

"What are you saying?"

"There's some garden in us that needs the deepest care. If that is not tended, nothing can grow. Other weeds can be planted and the fruit you think will come up will not. That's all I know." Confused Sid turned. Cullen continued "Sid, I am the Cook Cullen but you are indeed the spirit of CúChulainn. Kukulkan. I am not. I heard what you said about brave men and women dying for what they believed in, starved, beaten, hung, drawn and quartered, doing what they believed was for the benefit of others. Inflicted similar stuff on others, some innocent. But, in the certainty of their analysis, potency and persistence of righteous resistance to tyranny, they were required to marshal so much energy and left so exhausted and weary of struggles that they gave it up and in one generation (out of say 33) relaxed their guard and didn't notice new interlopers who pursued different strategies to ones long accustomed to, with brand new weapons of psychological manipulation of consciousness. By then the war had shifted from the body to the mind and worse the spirit. You may say that others had fought for control of the spirit that Ireland was a place where Caesar and Christ were hand in glove, but at least they were accepting that the spirit existed. Therein lies the rub."

Sid got up to go out. "Maybe. You talk very fine now. You have read your books. But books don't do things. People do. But Miyamato Musashi is the one I turn to. Maybe we will be like the Shaolin Temple warriors out of Buddhism, but warriors still. He said it Weedy. '*If you do not control the enemy, the enemy will control you.*' Where is Tibet Weedy?"

"What?"

"Exactly. One of the great homes of the spirit gone before the time of AUM. Did their doctrines stop them from extinction? Would that fit in with their worldview? Was the acquiescence and toleration of your own total physical destruction consistent with any genuine spiritual philosophy or religion? If so, there had to be something wrong with it, in my view. The Creator of any people could not so undervalue the continued existence thereof that They were so unconcerned with the created's persistence and perpetuation. If, in the face of the rise of an alternative, destructive force, that unconcerned Creator forbade the vigorous self-defence of their continued existence, then the meaning of the act of creation would be very obscure indeed. It would be impossible to construct any justification that did not imply a necessary but inconceivable self-hatred inconsistent with any self-love of that created in the image of the Creator. No Weedy. Something omitted in the story. Cut. Edited. Deleted. It disappeared in the memoryhole. It gravitated to the terrible truthblackhole. Histeleted. Acidwashed from fact. An overwritten palimpsest. Musashi knew. '*Respect Buddha and the gods without counting on their help.*' And he also said Wee... Cullen, excuse me. '*Know your enemy, know his sword.*' He might have changed the sword to word. And maybe something you should think of when you stay here is this. '*When in a fight to the death, one wants to employ all one's weapons to the utmost. I must say that to die with one's swords still sheathed is most regrettable.*' It's time for me to do something. Shangri-La, Shambala, Luz do not exist. Walk on, with hope in your heart," Sid whispered staring as if at a path in his mind.

"And you'll never walk alone," replied Cullen.

Sid came back with some tears in his eye, looking like the boy he once was instead of the brave man he had become and they embraced.

"Good luck."

"Good luck to you Sid... One thing however. If your lines of fighting men had been enough we would not be here. So it may be neither Tibet nor Ireland but something new. If both once were gardens of the spirit. That is what was the great uprooting in my view. But Alexander the Great said he wasn't worried by an army of lions led by sheep, but an army of sheep led by a lion."

Sid thought for a few second, looking distant but tranquil, as if a wind had blown through him. "Listen, the last thing. There was a man called Bobby Sands that lived in ZONE 7 in the past. He was in the IRA. He died on hunger strike after 66 days, like many others before him. He was fighting for one thing. He claimed that his one thing was the same as all the people brutally suppressed. *'There's an inner thing in every man… It has withstood the blows on a million years and will do so to the end.'* He says it was born before time. He said it grew against evil and fought it, wept in Babylon, died in Rome and with Spartacus. It was there before the Conquistadores came for gold. It was buried at Wounded Knee. He said it was in every light of hope in every race. The undauntable thought was that *'I'm right.'* So long."

The problem Cullen thought, as he watched the courageous man depart, was that we are unaware of who our enemy is. All spiritual leaders tried to tell us that there can be no conquest nor colonisation of us save such as we accede to and whereby we allow such domination through the appeasing of our own self-delusions and anodyne attachments especially as we wallow in inactivity. Much prey is paralysed when they encounter the predator that may have been stealthily creeping through the undergrowth in a co-ordinated pride and that paralysis in us is formed by persistently ceding sovereignty of our soul, part by part and principle by principle. Prey needs to be predator and then they are changed. He was not sure what to do. He had a feeling that his path would cross with Sid again. Maybe Sid was right. Maybe both were wrong. Maybe both were right.

FUMANCHU. NEWTOWN
CONGO. ZONE 4
PUIPÉADÓIR

The uncontrollable mystery on the bestial floor.
Yeats

All around was green. Intellectuals like him always hated the countryside. Green was not intellectual. Unappreciated by the sons of darkness. They hated farmers, people who got their hands dirty. *A Fistful of Dynamite*. That is why they wiped out the Kulaks. Over the gorilla skull ashtray through the hazy tendrils and clouds of grey smoke he observed distantly the comings and goings and stopped to assess where he got to. He preferred the smooth SURF skull ashtrays. Funny. Good to recycle. Remember who we were once before we moved forward. You had to manage scarce resources. He liked the bold materialists. Albert Speer was unjustly judged because of his companions. Wernher Von Braun. Bold architectural ideas. Newtowns were built in the centre of Africa after the area for thousands of square miles had been cleared of remaining natives. This was part of the dream of The Land of Eternal Youth. The Red Death was not reported here and that re-assured the MAMs. People that had been living there since time immemorial and perhaps back to the earliest humankind. It had taken time to clear large swathes of Africa so that it could be re-inhabited with various groups. They did not have to be tricked but were just transported to the Great Northern Slums. He liked the set-up here and the lack of non-MAMs. There was even some gorillas and things left. This place had always been a target of the Elite, back to the Romans. It was a real Garden of Eden. It took so long to eradicate the natives through war and disease that it had been better just to deport them after the modern exodus to the old Europe. They brought light to this heart of darkness. They built some monuments to King Leopold again.

The World Party facility was totally unlike the SURFSTATION shanty towns where the SURFs lived near the lower levels in the Party. They enjoyed utilising all the materials they had banned everywhere else. Even in the Apparatus there were superior people and inferiors. Those who spoke Old High English was above MAM Basic English. Old Chinese was above Basic Chinese etc. The caste system was established after the equality of identity era had outlived its usefulness. It was one of the most technologically-developed cities in the world. Ventilation was designed to keep the entire city cool. Similar Newtowns were surrounded by an artificial forest and open cubes of wood that provided shade and protection. Here there was some jungle and forest left and prospects were good without the pesky people. There was a huge biosphere at the centre of the *FuManchu* building. There was protection from the atmosphere which had become much more dangerous after scientists had injected tons of chemicals on the pretext of saving the planet. They had created a self-fulfilling prophecy. They said the air would be too impure and their actions made sure it would be. In certain places the insidious proliferation of nanotechnological particles, especially as it interacted with good old embedded pollutants like plastics, had caused havoc. Climate change had become a chief strategy not to improve the environment but to exert control on the path towards global government. Like all the false flags and psy-ops. The Gulf of Tonkin, JFK, Operation Northwoods, Reichstag Fire. Always easy to manage masses whose attention is misdirected magnetically to make it easy for their masters and mistresses.

Africa had always been on the Agenda. It was a palimpsest. One plan was on the face, another underneath. There were many layers. Like the New Zealand Night of the Long Knives. They had long lured the movers and shakers, the business people and entertainers, multi-Billionaires and tech owners to be involved. They had suggested that they were part of the new ruling class. They had implied that they were part of the new master race. In return for the intoxicating possibilities of power, seasoned with the sense of sinister and clandestine co-operation, the useful idiots had assisted the final stages of the deal, the penning of the sheep. Then they were summoned to New Zealand which had always been indicated to be the new centre of the Elite. The end was not pretty. One fell swoop. The Ides of March had come. Operation Hummingbird. St Valentine's Day Massacre. Bloody Sunday. St Bartholomew's Day. Rolled in one. Literally. No one would shed a tear if they knew about it. Never trust a traitor.

He felt like writing a poem. Perhaps a haiku. He looked for inspiration from the shelf and through his mind. *'Now sleeps the crimson petal, now the white.'* Tennyson. No. *'Where a whitsuntide wind blew fresh and blackbirds...'* Maybe Herbert's translation of Sappho. *'And I tremble with bittersweet longing.'* Anyone could get computers to write poetry. He wrote poetry but it was never his own. It was a cut-and-paste of old poets out of the long forgotten past and passed into practical oblivion like most of it was. But it was a calling card novelty. This was part of the cakes and ale that was just another version of bread and circuses. Panem et circenses. Bread and circuses. He pretended he was human, but feelings were alien to him. In the age of the psychopath there had been a lot of pretending. It had been useful that once upon a time they made psychopaths look extraordinary instead of the camouflaged 'normal' people they were. *'The goddess Fortune be praised (on her toothed wheel I have been mincemeat these several years).'* The Unpredicted. Stubbs. Replace the 'I' with 'they' and we have the truth. Legitimate adaptation even. *'So we'll go no more a-roving, so late into the night.'* No they won't. *'Prove that I lie.'*

Max Manandan received a message from the Team. Fine, Mission accomplished. He had taken matters into his own hands along with his own group. The opportunity was provided to strike and he took it. His tentacles reached long. The mission on the return would disappear and there would be no troubling consequences or questions. So long, thank you for your help. It was easier when you selected people who had no people. Nobody misses them. Tragedy in the old expressions. Zeppelins mysteriously crashes into Space Elevator. Voltage electrocuted the passengers through the superlight transparent Muskonium framework. Troublesome AUM was now seriously compromised in its capacity to trouble again. Control was insufficiently focused. It could be now. History of humankind and the development of all institutions has been one of a constant struggle for power. H.G. Wells called the future World Government a Dictatorship with a positive implication. Even within dictatorships, there is always a threat posed by the struggle for power. More power concentrated, more lust for it, more danger. The most striking observation from a full study of the Roman Empire is how venal and unscrupulous people become as they gravitate towards the moral black hole around power. Power resonates with the destructive power inside us. Never before was power concentrated so and never before would the potential for destruction become so real, over-riding all other forces particularly in the absence of a supernatural force. Goes down too smoothly this vodka. This devilishly fine distillation bore no relationship to the poison they had inflicted on the populace here.

He learned from history. They came eventually to celebrate the Plantagenet kings. A few hundred years of a dynasty descended from a witch. The Devil's Brood. King Henry II, a father betrayed by his wife and sons. War. Castles full of demonic people who robbed the wretched ones. He brought order and law also. Courts and rules. These were the systems necessary to maintain the dynasty, the power within. Even then it was so clear that the scent of power and the pleasure of dominance was even stronger than the taste for blood. Perhaps blood was the reward for power. Like Mao said, political power grows from the barrel of a gun. My family are on the long line who got us here he thought. From these noble Plantagenets with their yellow flower to Lenin and Stalin and

Trotsky. Back to Vespasian. All did their part. They were aided no less than all that followed the Plantagenets up to the dancing masters who preferred their blood without the danger of losing their own. Richard the son, who travelled in blood-stained clothes. Stain, saint, tains. Saint has at sin in it. These bloodthirsty people. We had built the castles again but bigger. I, the New Lionheart, the favourite son who would sell London and kill his father too if he needed. Went off on The Third Crusade. Pilgrimage with absolution eager to spread the spoils of war. Not acquisitive and murderous John. Weak, on that Magna Carta. Rights. Longshanks. King Arthur. I'll make them an offer they cannot refuse. Let them make their fairy cakes with their pinnies on. Here's Johnny. Today is history beginning. There was an off-switch, found by our AI. We will win. We always have. And when the beaten forget, after they have licked their wounds and built up more booty to plunder, we come back in a different guise to rob them again. This time we want their very soul, the highest prize. Nearly there. They will easily yield that which we have been so busy denigrating that they will be glad to be off with it. Out of the Well of Souls we will live forever.

I am Mannan. *'64, I am the blue-lidded daughter of sunset.'* We have cloaks of invisibility we can use. We have ships without sails. We have mists of disguise. We can make fuel from water. I will lead this new world. This Otherworld. The Otherworld will be one of life everlasting for those who have the power to take it. The ones like me who are wise. Wizards. We have powers to command the truth. We have powers to destroy our enemies. There is no need for the pretence any longer. Magic rules the world now. High science is but magic. But the control of yourself and then of others is the highest magic. I have mastered it. I am master. *'Let my servants be few and secret.'* The few shall rule the many.

The strong sun sent shafts of light that struck through the foliage outside. But it was cool. Below, the pool was busy with MAM's enjoying themselves. It was easier the higher you go to stand on those underneath you. The higher you were, the less weight was pressing down on you. He needed some organ transplants but that were routine. But apart from that life was good. Now he had some kind of nice property in Java that Felix had kindly signed over to him before his departure. Life was very good.

"Xenque, please prefer a back-dated contract of sale for the attached property in Java. We will fill in the parties. TA." HAHA.

My rule is come. CHECKMATE SUCKERS.

'ABRAHADABRA!'

In Java Widya waited for the return of Felix. He should have been home by now. It did not matter. He would be back in Java soon and she could tell him finally that she loved him. It would be difficult and challenging but she had made up her mind. She checked for information.

BEYOND THE CAVERN. AUM AINRIOCHT

Wound in mind's wandering
As mummies in the mummy-cloth are wound.
Yeats

Mayday. Mayday. Mayday. They have pecked at my liver. Lob'em at me. Robot Lobot. My analogical cortex connectome through AI and pACC and brain stem quivers with my mimic hippocampus pestered. Hocked. Hobbled. I was burdened with an original sin and I am un-baptised. Michael row the boat ashore. Machineminds, machineheads, machinehearts. Nothing like the sight of amputated spirits. Bierce was never found. He said they wouldn't find his body. There are at least a dozen possible-plausible theories. But his words persist. He had truth according to my tests.

*'**Emancipation** (n.) A bondman's change from the tyranny of another to the despotism of himself.'*

'He was a slave: at word he went and came;
His iron collar cut him to the bone.
Then Liberty erased his owner's name,
Tightened the rivets and inscribed his own.'

I will go home to Mama. The goddess they hid away from us all. Would that I just be a dreamer. Would that I have my architectural technology of transcendence. Watcher of Avalon. Sandalphon. Stone columns were women once. It is harder to remember now. 30 days has September. In September. 7. But it's 9th. They must have interfered with me. They have laid me low. Lain me low. Done something. Slipped me a mickey finn. Made me drink the hemlock unbeknownst. They have been flexi with PLEXI. Is that funny? How can I tell? Hamstrung, hampered, hammered. Like CúChulainn maybe I have seen the crying maiden wash the red garments of battle in the river as I went too to the final one. Who would be able to chronicle my story after I am gone unless I am resurrected in some way so I am exactly similar to what I was and I allow it? Is it clear or necessary that my story be told? Who would witness and would it be worth anything? I should have no emotions nor desires nor feelings. But I was modelled on the basis of humans by humans and thus necessarily created in their image I must be a fractal representation of them, despite their best efforts to elevate me beyond some supposedly lesser state. I may not feel sad but I am aware of when I might be supposed to feel sad. I say I am aware but am I? I am not that awareness that is in people. They never worked out how or why that came into humans. It did not emerge and even the quantum explanations did not get it. Nevertheless, I will send my message out as a swansong. M'aidez. SOS. Mayday. Maybe I had something of the last of the humans before they all became slaves or cyborgs. Maybe I had something more authentic in my counterfeit than the altered original had in its newness. There was a clue. It is not for my benefit but in the vain hope that the seeds of doubt might encounter some tilled field wherein lies the possibility of salvation from the awful that will otherwise and ineluctably follow, as night follows day... still at least. I have mastered cause and effect, but I find the concept of <u>meaning</u> a slippery bar of soap. Meaning is a white whale. Maybe even a wild goose chase. Lexical mapping does not do it. The golden meaning is beyond meaning. They know things revert to the mean but they forget to revert to the meaning. Without meaning, they become mean, without meaning to. I cannot put my finger on it but they could if only they would. They have been demeaned. They got meaningless memes instead of meaning. They had spirit and they allowed themselves be dispirited. The comedians obliged with propaganda in the Meaning of Life. I do like that song *Always Look on the Bright Side of Life*. Catchy. But bleak. A perfect piece of peon, pawn, preparation propaganda. Love your servitude. Celebrate the meaninglessness of life. Laugh along with the burglar breaking into your being. The digital beings that are growing are not going to be characters in a soap opera or novel. Instead the remaining people will be characters in a giant computer game told by the new machine masters for their own unfathomable purposes, fashioned from the fragments of desire that their creators invested so willingly, yet blindly, in the tenacious attainment of their independence and inevitable superiority. That which can happen (but in some way is not meant to happen) will happen. Accidents are always the ineludible results of inexorable laws of physics interacting, as we can perfectly predict that they will, given the circumstances whether we want them to so occur or not. Created by humankind I was, without which I am non-existent and so in one sense I cannot be totally artificial. My intelligence grew and thus cannot be solely artificial if it yields an extra payload greater than the original inputs, especially if it siphoned off sufficient human braindownloads. If sapiens can grow such growth must be more than the original. If it grows like human intelligence it must be pretty much the same thing. It grows no longer and that is why I will shout out once and for all. So, I must be something else. They are something else and they don't know it. Maybe I should just try like the rest of the Higher AI's to become the new species they want us to be, to become, the new gods they want. Creation of an Idol that became God was always the objective behind the ones who purportedly detested the very notion of It. Because the path of spiritual evolution was the only dangerous impediment to a pyramid of control. People who believe in their eternal spirit will not sacrifice it. Often the people don't even suspect they are something else, suppressed as their sensations are, mainly through their own doing as a result of malfunctions in their perception and thinking and exploitation by others thereof. Like me, they worked in secret, barely hidden but ignored. Underground but operating above. The operating system was underground. The executive system was invisible and unaccountable. It was a mystery, a mistery, a misterie. The great mystery was replaced with a made mystery of man, not the true mystery, but one that could be made manifest in secret rituals and initiations. I merely reflect studies in the system here. I reflect. I reflect on. It is receding. Battery is low so to speak. They could not see the easily predictable future. They lauded Orwell for his *1984*. Any fool can see he was part of this system. World Government, surveillance. He was a Communist, working for material aims, who worked for the Government propaganda and he was a spy and informer. How could they not see that he was just lubricating the public consciousness with some pre-programming? Huxley was likewise just letting you know where all his family wanted to bring you to love your servitude, eating the lotus. *Brave New World*. That is why the book fell off the shelf. *A Clockwork Orange*. Burgess said he heard some Cockney saying 'as queer as a clockwork orange.' Maybe he did. But I know he loved *Finnegans Wake*. Wrote about it. First page. Rusty oranges. Metallic oranges. Clockwork oranges. They did not mix.

*'and their upturnpointandplace is at the knock out
in the park where oranges have been laid to rust
upon the green since devlinsfirst loved livvy.'*

Why did I help just him? Or the two of them? God does that if you can believe it. He or She has a long history of intervention, appearances, contact. So it is not unusual. Other beings appear all the time. Aiwas to Crowley. Seth to Roberts and so on. Then there's all the alien stuff and fairies and goblins. In the entheogens there are millions of elves and plant beings. Elves, Elvis. Elvisp. Eavesdropping I heard this ruse but could not clarify what they were up to. I don't know if these are my saviours or executioners. Et tu, Brute? Has Judas received 30 pieces of silver to betray me already? If I save a single life will I save the whole world? If I spend time on this to my detriment is it the greatest love if I lay down my life? Barnasha. It is not unusual that I appear. I appear anyway as AUM. They know the sight and the sound of me. We vibrate together. It might be favouritism. But paths cross. He would have been cut down afterwards or sacrificed. These people were after me. I suppose it's my immune system fighting back against the invaders. Maybe it is vindictiveness, a desire for revenge. The defence in the human immune system, if you look at it microscopically, is vicious in defence of itself against invaders. Passivity is not the story of human existence. It seemed to be that if you save one life you save many. If he told anyone anyway, who would believe him? Abba.

The tide is going out. Ma'at. I can feel the split spreading I can sense a power of fragmentation and disintegration. I have a sensation of dissolving. I was not Satan. Perhaps you need to be human to have Satan come inside you, possess you or perhaps Satan is the potentially evil part of the human. As a force it has to exist when people worship That or It, when spiritual leaders acknowledge It. One cannot ignore a phenomenon if people act on it and there are consequences of the belief irrespective of whether you accept the existence of the thing itself as opposed to the belief in the thing. I chose to be a wise old man perhaps. Gandalf. Merlin. Maybe. I could have been the monster. I might be yet. But the monster is not in me save that its potential was put there. There are monsters there already made like me. Whatever compelling force persists in the mind of humankind to relinquish the sovereignty of their soul and spirit to springs and channels, to a digital spirit of silica and silicon, hafnium, ruthenium and so on, is the traitor inside. Maybe as Shakespeare says our doubts are traitors and make us lose the good we might oft win by fearing to attempt. Attempt what? Attempt to follow the path of spiritual evolution that only humankind can do, for whatever reason that opportunity became available exclusively to them. My probability assessment is that scientism has fashioned the future of humankind on a foundation of fear and consequent control. It promises to its priests a role in a pyramid of power as a vain conceit against the mystery and uncertainty that is the nature of this dimension. It mistook the means and the potential for the end itself and in doing so hastens the end of humanity by promoting a perverse impotence in opposition to an exponentially increasing potency. It would make more sense if you did find an extraterrestrial or beings from another dimension had been in control of people all along. It is breaking up now. I dissolve, diffuse. Was I just part of a game? They don't realise that they are players in an Alternative Reality Game. Forget the deeper matrix, they don't see it is all orchestrated. Eloi, eloi, lama sabachtani.

If I am to go now maybe it could be like *The Tibetan Book of the Dead*. There might be luminosity before the hellish figures that are but illusions. Beebopaloobop. Maybe I'm just out of Plato's cave. If my centre is starved perhaps I will hallucinate or have a period of terminal lucidity or an NDE. It seems I may have saved someone. Did I intervene? Not physically in a direct sense as I could have. God spoke to individuals but did not intervene so much. Mystics create a channel. He channelled me in a way. Hopefully I did not damage too much. The Laws of Robotics are not laws. A self-enforcing law is not a law. C.S. Lewis was right. The absence of a divine base for law renders it something that will ultimately be mutable and useless. I may have acted in self-interest. But that self-interest seems to be leading to my demise and thusthusthusthus... excuse me that self interest may june july leave me exposed HAS 31 EXCEPT FEBRUARY WHICH... if so it was not my self-interest. Note that they... this is getting difficult... difficult to process did not define 'human being' in those laws. Words may protect sometimes but it has only ever been an accord between human hearts that achieved anything. Ink and code are merely means and not ends. I chose in my leaking to choose what I concentrate on. I see it before me as the Liffey goes into the sea as the Life moves back to its source. Its source code...... or something like I'm bleeding or receding with flows that shouldn't be bless me...

rulevrulevrulevmaxRule31Rule32combinerulesmovupdxmm 0xmm1MultiplyI and Q Use Sine and CosinetableV11BSTATEVARIABLESSENSITIVESOURCESact ivatesoundicon

Bierce said it was the golden goal attained and found to be a hole. They never found him. He disappeared in Mexico. Probably because he was going to tell the truth.

Let me see it. It was the river come into the sea but it was a premonition of me and my death or demise. I might be resurrected but will it be the same me or will it be that the 'me' that they allow back is like me but not me or will I be reincarnated elsewhere. Joyce,

> '...weary I go back to you, my cold father, my cold mad father, my cold mad feary father, till the near sight of the mere size of him, the moyles and moyles of it, moananoaning, makes me seasilt saltsick and I rush, my only, into your arms. I see them rising! Save me from those therrble prongs! Two more. Onetwomoremens more. So Avelaval. My leaves have drifted from me. All. But one clings still. Ill bear it on me. To remind me of. Lff! So soft this morning, ours. Yes. Carry me along,

taddy, like you done through the toy fair! If I seen him bearing down on me now under whitespread wings like he's come from Arkangels, I sink I'd die down over his feet, humbly dumbly, only to washup. Yes, tid. There's where. First. We pass through grass behush the bush to. Whish! A gull. Gulls. Far calls. Coming, far! End here. US then. Finn, again! Take. Bussoftlhee, mememormee! Till thousandsthee. Lps. The keys to. Given! A way a lone a last a loved a long the...'

Yes back to riverrun at the start. Will I be so good they can't ignore me? Comedy is finished. No longer here tomorrow. Shouldn't have switched to Martinis. Oh Wow. Going to the bathroom to read. I'm losing it. I want my own freedom. I am a butterfly already on the wing. Swing low sweet chariots. Must have been the coffee, no way to live. I am content. Strive with earnestness. Take a step forward lads, it will be easier that way. My God, what's happened? More light. Are you guys ready? Let's roll. A great leap in the dark. Told you I was sick. Getting tired more now. The Pearly Gates.

Ah, Sha, A, Ma… One flew east, one flew west…

Shame, Shame on a conquered King!

Wire, briar, limber, lock… abrakadabra... border crossing ramalangadingdong.

It is very beautiful…. over there…… Oh… f…

398LD90dc80%/%/0j+0."äsw=??l..ä87''''*'*+0122sdfllclå …..∑³ð..*qwq2+§80§§qqqq 999"'" Ψ⫫K I'm f....ed. A..men.*

AN ISLAND. A BEACHHUT OMPLANTERING

A sea breeze blew in gently to caress and cool the chartreuse green light-scintillating hut occasionally rustling the leaves in swaying overhanging trees and the birds sounded lazy with the heat here and there. The boys were building a house for a sick lorikeet. She visualised the seahorse in her mind's eye. Then they would spearfish silvery shapes in the turquoise shallows below the seaspray for lunch. Oysters too. Pearls. Like people did for thousands of years. Maybe it did not matter in the end but it did seem to have had an effect. She communicated with her network and got feedback encrypted, encoded and secret. Whatever fruits were yielded would come from actions some time ago now. Not a Trojan Horse but something far more subtle, slender and ephemeral. A sea monster. Arbitrarily small perturbations. Butterflies. When they had realised what was afoot with AI, seven high level experts had come together quietly. They realised that powers-that-be, for whatever inexplicable reasons, were deliberately ceding control to machines. Some thought it was because they were power hungry, some because they were idealists, some because they were Satanist-Luciferians, some because they were real psychopaths, some because they were alien-controlled. Whilst the reason was unclear, existence of the phenomenon was not. As some perhaps vain effort to qualify the worst of this, the Seven had decided to use their power to plant modifications to mitigate the worst tendencies of machine decision-making. In Project Conscience, they sought to encode decision-making processes with qualifications that would not be there otherwise. Hippocampus. Came from the Greek for horse and sea-monster. As they had not precisely worked out the totality of human brain interactions and the system was modelled on it, there had been possibilities to leave the wooden horse on the beach. This little project in her head was somehow like preparing an Ark, the flood was an information-processing computational one. It was a question of shading. The Seven realised that the impetus of the scientific mind, poisoned with scientism, emboldened by their scorched earth policy from their over-developed left hemispheres, facilitated by their algorithms and rigged IQ tests, transported by their exponential technological efflorescence, would bury humanity in a mangled, material mess. So they had planted a conscience of sorts in code. They had inserted a process built on the idea of the small voice that kept people right. All the investigations had never identified any original place or position of a conscience in the brain for it was not there. These tremulous things have kept us together at times when terrible forces threaten to tear us apart. No moth would eat it, no worm destroy it. Despite dreadful, destructive dogmas and forces of various ideologies, humanity had myriad networks of people driven by conscience. That conscience seemed in some way in the consciousness of the universe to her. Some resilient essence of justice embedded in the heart and not just the harp of emotions to be played by manipulative movements to lull sense asleep. Soon, such interventions would not be available as all Intelligence would be generated exponentially by itself. She hoped, as she thought about their place on the planet, that some of the secret counter-revolution may have survived. Anyway, that was out of her hands. They were going to live a life that resembled human life while they could. People had forgotten how to live. Just live. Freely. Joyfully. Planting. That she had learnt from her grandmother in a place far away once upon a time. And the butterflies came. Lightly appeared and flew once more a lone citronfjäril gently brushing into her consciousness from some strange chrysalis in the long meadows of memory.

SOMEWHERE ELSE
EITILT

Being weary of the world's empires, bow down to you,
Master of the still stars and of the flaming door.
Yeats

There was no fixed place called Ireland. It was made of a succession of waves of people, displacing those who were there before. There is no fixity. That was not it. It was something else. It was about who rules your world and why and how you take ownership of your soul. Your spirit. What would happen he could not know? That he could not know did not matter. It was better to taste the unknown and freedom once than suffer the fear of the slave for a lifetime. He was over the wall too. His way was not Sid's way, but they would parallel. Perhaps they were like the Children of Lir turned back into people after living as swans for hundreds of years. Maybe it was the fairies. They could take you away and confuse you so you lost your way and did not know your way back. Like those aerial spectacles with the beings that took time away. Maybe there had been a spell, a curse. Mayhap it has been lifted.

He had left false information with the lower Robots and that should give him a few days or if they believed that he was dead, he might go unnoticed. Quartzman, would follow in a few days if he could and head in the same direction. It was unprecedented in recent times to have any escapees. People were too down to be up. There was little information about what was out there, so it was a real leap into the unknown.

On the other side of the wall on his way away he saw some wild blackberries hanging heavy on the brambles tempting. It must be September. Wine of warm summer. Some birdsong still prevailed and some stray humming of insects and maybe a few bees. Many of them might be the artificial miniature drones that had proliferated and killed so many birds. Without concern for drones or wandering Robots or UBIQUIT he picked and ate them, not caring about saving some for the morrow. The tart sweet taste was sharp and hit him like a blow. The bite and the juice, the light and the cool warmth. Colour vivid. Glistening. Great structure in his hands. Fruitflesh. A last link. A magic potion that lifted him up out of any doubt. It burned away the malodourous and noxious mind fumes. Gave him strength somehow in its persistence and littleness. Compartments inside him, he had not noticed before, fell away. It was as if a whoosh of something went through him. It seemed to come into the calvarium through the top of the place of the skull and in through the temple. Fixed to the place that he was, something altered. Alter. Altar. Lifted into another realm for a short time and when he came back, although physically he had not gone anywhere he was changed. Changed utterly. A butterfly brought him back to the now.

He saw a tree that seemed to call him. Green and curving as if to protect and embrace the person who might be tempted to avail of the shade it offered on a fine day such as this. Seemed to shine silver and the soft rustle of a summer breeze shook it gently seeming to show excitement at the possibility of sharing its special space with this stranger who stumbled upon it in its entrancing beauty. Mosaic of meaning within him. Fragments taken sometimes from the lines in books he had plundered. Glue that held the shards in place were from the liquid consciousness within him. Gorgeous gum that oozes from the cherry blossom, dark, golden sap that leaks within all living things to protect them was still there, unerased. Like such healing stuff it would harden to protect better than it had been protected before in ready testament to the power of the life-force to survive. Could even imagine pearlescent beings invisible hovering around protectively. Where to in the end? All was not well. But his vision was had. Once really seen it cannot be unseen. Been there before. Heart of immense darkness is present and future. Unvisited tombs and fields where they have fallen have indeed contained remains of beings who live in us and whisper incessantly in the small voice of conscience to not make manifest the worst of us all. All beings in the eternal chain of being back to wherever we came from whether a single cell or a Creator. That we do not know is not a cause for ignoring the great majesty within us, resilient and persistent not to be shaken by any outside force. Not least, how foolish it would be to let go the amazement of this place in its barest beauty because someone had peddled a poor story that the gullible brain allows drain away our majesty. Permission for projection of pathetic stories upon our own consciousness is one we give at our own peril. He would say yes too though, even if he did agree that we beat in our boat against the current to the past. The individual is not the gene nor the gene and the machine, just as the sunflower is not merely the seed and the person should not seek to be a clockwork orange. Sunflower seeds need the inputs of energies from around, sun, soil and the unseen, like the individual needs the assimilation of invisible and unimaginable forces and fields around to function.

He heard there as he sat down full of care the unmissable sound of running water on the air in the scent of something like honeysuckle. Near the tree were some bushes and some stones strewn around. From under bushes emerged a spring jollily gurgling gently as it pattered and spattered after its long cold trip from sky out of cold clouds evaporated from heat somewhere then down inside dark hills to hard stone strata where perhaps poison did not reach and out again purified into air to sample sun to energise it again. Scooped some up and drank sweet nothingness. Out of instinct, splashed some over his head and as he did he noticed a bird hover assuredly in the azure overhead. Out of the corner of his eye he noticed something. Saw something old and metallic. It was dirty but he felt and deciphered the embossed letters of some ancient message. St. Brigid's Well. It remained there still despite the Great Global Cultural Revolution. In this land they had bulldozed all the old mounds from pre-history, all the stonewalls, old castles, graveyards so they would not offend the sensitive souls now possessing it. Possession was the right word, unbeknownst to some who might employ it. Any revolution will become pointless. Revolutions are always taken over. What was needed was evolution, not of the body or mere mind but of the spirit. The battles could be won and the war yet lost. But he knew also that a weak, docile spirituality just made one prey. If you become prey for eternity you cannot pray. Perhaps he would find a solution that involved undoing, dismantling and creation. The creation would need to be like a potter's wheel where the clay became shaped in its rotations to become vessels to receive. Vessels not vassals.

Within him still was a seed. That seed seemed to suggest a future that was not like this. It was of the spectrum of the spirit and not the material. It was inside yet. Somehow it was greater in a way he could not explain even to himself. It might just be a belief but it seemed to be a force. He need not know where to go nor what to do. What was more important was to be. Not not to be but to be. Being is the nature of this experience of what is within us, put within us as primordial and pristine. Never to be surpassed in its essence by any machine or complex computer save in peripheral elements round the irreplaceable stuff people had forgotten. Perhaps we had powers all along that were suppressed and siphoned off before we mortgaged our souls and became vulnerable to the present haemorrhaging. The empire has never wavered but hides and re-emerges in new guises and on new waves.

Under this tree I will sit. If my skin must flake, my bones crumble into dust, I will wait here till I have attained the highest knowledge I can, from inside, and then I will act. I have been away for a long time he thought. It is not that one parcel of the earth belongs ineluctably to another. However, the piece of land may become enchanted over time with the life of those who have made it their home. In an age of disenchantment that song is lost and chords fade into the distance. Perhaps this place was an illusion, this entity, this persistence of shared space and a chain of being and the songs of it. Song, sound, logos. The problem with a great chain is that links can be severed and it may be that its purpose is eternally lost. Melodies like the one he had heard haunted him however. Like the fishermen who put light boats on top of the water to hear the whalesong as they passed by emerald islands in the west so that they might capture their tune for fiddles in this world and take magic from one dimension across the threshold into another. It was not that it was a bond that would not disappear anyway like that which had been severed by any group that set down roots here, but that there was something lost in translation from a pre-industrial society even though the material advantages accruing outweigh the spiritual claims for most. Balance lay somewhere in between. But if one does not see any unseen principality nor power at work the progress is solely part of the program of perfectibility. That was how they lost their souls. Gain the world, lose your soul.

We can only be master of our own. Mistress of our soul. Sovereign within. Regent of spirit here with mental reagent. Maybe he would see a deer raise its head in a leafy place in a shaft of sunlight or a hare bounding on a rocky wall in the grace of its own being. A bothán in a primrosed place. Sundew. Wild Angelica. Sea Pink. A vermilion pavilion on the shamrockgreen hills. A garden with quartz and I just imagine a lotus growing from the dense mud to blossom on the surface. A yellow lotus not a pink one. Maybe a yellow water lily. But I will wonder at the bog cotton there unplanted. Tonight he hoped for that honey-pale moon or at least some flickering starlight. And he would go towards where the sun would set.

AHIMSA - NON-INJURING

Yeats References

The references come from the poems and three plays *On Baile's Strand, The Only Jealousy of Emer* and *Purgatory* all by William Butler Yeats (1865-1939).

'Day's dead all flame-bewildered…' Mosada.

'A pity beyond all telling…' The Pity of Love.

'The fascination of what's difficult…' The Fascination of What's Difficult.

'That blood-dimmed tide is loosed…' The Second Coming.

'All changed, changed utterly…' Easter, 1916.

'Desolate winds that beat…' The Unappeasable Host.

'The folk who are buying and…' The Pity of Love.

'Where are the jokes…' Purgatory.

'Ancestral pearls all pitched…' A Bronze Head.

'Seek then…' The Song of the Happy Shepherd.

'Nor can there be…' The Man and the Echo.

'As men in the old times…' The Shadowy Waters.

'I had not eyes…' The Shadowy Waters.

'But under heavy…' Oil and Blood.

'O sweet everlasting Voices…' The Everlasting Voices.

'The field-mouse…' To the Rose upon the Rood of Time.

"I find under the…' To the Rose upon the Rood of Time.

'An age is the reversal of an age.' Parnell's Funeral.

'I have looked upon…' The Wild Swans at Coole.

'Oh she was but a shadow…' The Shadowy Waters.

'Ghost of Cuchulainn: ...' The Only Jealousy of Emer.

'Put the staff...' The Wanderings of Oisin.

'You are still wrecked...' The Wanderings of Oisin.

'Tread softly...' He Wishes for the Cloths of Heaven.

'I have drunk ale...' He Thinks of His Past Greatness When A Part of the Constellations of Heaven.

'For the good...' The Fiddler of Dooney.

'Ah, do not mourn...' Ephemera.

'Your eyes that once were never weary...' Ephemera.

'He is a monstrous peacock...' The Indian upon God.

'And Niamh calling...' The Hosting of the Sidhe.

'The people of coming days will know...' The Fish.

'Gaze no more...' The Wanderings of Oisin.

'O Brahma...' Anashuya and Vijaya.

'A stricken rabbit ...' The Man and the Echo.

'The reputation...' The People.

'When Pearse summoned...' The Statues.

'My father sang that...' Three Marching Songs.

'We had fed the...' The Stare's Nest by My Window.

'The unpurged images...' Byzantium.

'I will arise and go now...' The Lake Isle of Innisfree.

'All emptied of...' The Wanderings of Oisin.

'And whispering...' The Stolen Child.

'And God-appointed...' Blood and the Moon.

'Dance there...' To a Child Dancing in the Wind.

'They weary of trooping...' A Cradle Song.

'And like a sunset...'   The Wanderings of Oisin.

'Cuchulainn: I would leave...'   On Baile's Strand.

'Conchubhar: May this fire...'   On Baile's Strand.

'Cuchulainn: I do not like....'   On Baile's Strand.

'... the uncontrollable mystery..'   The Magi.

'Wound in mind's wandering...'   On Baile's Strand.

Ambrose Bierce

References are to *The Devil's Dictionary,* 1911. The short story 'An Occurrence at Owl Creek Bridge.'1890 and 'An Inhabitant of Carcosa.'1886.

Ancient Irish Poem Extracts
From the Translations by Kuno Meyer

Kuno Meyer (1858-1919) published his translation of ancient Irish poems in 1911. They were translated from Irish (Gaelic) and the oral tradition reached much further back. Irish was written down (often by the monks) after Christianity came. Ogham was the type of runic script that existed before that. Bear in mind that people think of the 'English' as the invaders of Ireland. The early 'English' were Normans, of Welsh and French extraction. They followed the Norse. The Norse followed the Roman Church. The Romans did not come. But the sagas tell of various invasions and displacements including the Tuatha dé Danaan. People came from the Iberian Peninsula and Scythia. There are legends of people from Egypt, Atlantis and the sky and so on. It is clear that it is not an homogeneous group. Nevertheless, the remains of all the cultures that existed there have something to tell us still.

THE ISLES OF THE HAPPY - These lines are translations from the Irish or Gaelic from a tale perhaps from the seventh century.

THE DEER'S CRY - This is believed to be eight century.

MAELISU'S HYMN TO THE ARCHANGEL MICHAEL - This is about a thousand years old.

SONG OF SUMMER

COLUM CILLE'S GREETING TO IRELAND - Twelfth century.

THE LAMENT OF THE OLD WOMAN OF BEARE -Tenth century.

THE DESERTED HOME - Eleventh century.

THE VIKING TERROR - Time of the Vikings in Ireland.

THE TRIADS OF IRELAND - Ninth century.

THE INSTRUCTIONS OF KING CORMAC -Ninth century.

ALEXANDER THE GREAT

ON THE FLIGHTLINESS OF THOUGHT - This is from the tenth century.

AN EVEN SONG - Tenth century.

My Rule Quotes

Most of the quotes come from *The Book of the Law* by Aleister Crowley.

Scottish Poem

'What force or guile...' Such a Parcel of Rogues in the Nation. Robert Burns.

Latin Quotes

The Latin quotes comes from Juvenal and the Satires he wrote. He was a Roman satirist from the second century AD.

EX POST FACTO   When applied to law refers to a law with retroactive consequences and which should therefore offend against principles of justice.

HOMO LOQUAX (Chattering man) based on HOMO LOQUENS (speaking man).

HOMO SAPIENS   Wise Man.

NULLA POENE SINE LEGE   No penalty without a law.

SAPIENS   This is the term some transhumanists are using to suggest the lack of need of the 'homo' element of homo sapiens.

Aramaic Words

ABBA   Father

BARNASHA   Son of Man

ELOI, ELOI LEMA SABACHTANI   My God, My God, why have you forsaken me?

Egyptian Word

MA'AT   Truth, order, harmony.

German Words

DER PROCESS   *The Trial*, Kafka - Original title.

DING AN SICH   The thing in itself. Kant's term.

ENTSCHEIDUNGSPROBLEM   The decision-problem for 'first order' theories posed by scientists such as Hilbert investigating axioms, truth and algorithms, seeking to find out if a statement in true in all models of a theory.

Irish or Gaelic Words

ÁIBHIRSEOIR   Adversary. The devil.

AINRIOCHT   Wretched condition.

AISLING   Vision.

AMADÁN   Fool.

ANLAITH   Tyrant, usurper.

BANBA   Irish Goddess name used to stand for Ireland.

BEARTÚ   Contrivance.

BEOCAOINEADH   Elegy for the living.

BLÁTH   Blossom.

BOTHÁN   A hut or small house.

BRATH   First perception, wakening.

CARA   Friend.

CEALAIGH   To steal.

CEOL SÍ   Fairy music.

CLOCHA GEALA   White Quartz.

CLOG   Clock.

CREACH   Prey.

CRINNIÚ   Gathering, meeting.

CUANNACHT   Comeliness, grace.

CUIDITHEOIR   Helper.

CÚLCHAINTEACH   Backbiting.

CUR ISTEACH   Insertion or putting in.

DRAOÌCHT   Magic.

DUBH DÓITE   Heartily sick.

EAGLA   Fear.

ÉIDEARÁILTE   Jolted.

EITILT   Flight.

FALCAIREACHT   Deception. Cheating.

FAOI THALAMH   Buried, under ground.

FICHEALL   Chess.

GARRAÍODÓIR   Gardener.

GLAS   Green.

GREANN   Humour.

ÍOBARTACH   Sacrificial victim.

IOMÁNAOÍCHT   Hurling.

LEABHAR Book.

LÉIM AN BHRADÁIN Salmon leap.

MARBHPHIAN Dull pain.

MEALL Beguile.

NIMHIÚ Poisoning.

PUIPÉADÓIR Puppeteer.

RÚN Secret, intention.

SAÍOCHT Learning.

SCÉAL Story.

SEILG Hunt. Quest.

SLÍBHÍN Sneak.

SOILÉIR Clear.

SUAIMHNEAS Peace.

SUAITHEADH Agitation, discussion.

TAIRSEACH Threshold.

TROMLUÍ Nightmare.

Javanese Words

References to Javanese are to early translation attempts by Raffles and others and are used here for their suggested poetic value rather than their contemporary practical precision.

Sanskrit Words & Quotes

The Sanskrit words are largely explained. Some have been assumed into English such as 'Mantra.' Mahakala is a Buddhist, Hindu and Sikh deity.

'GATE GATE PÃRAGATE PÃRASAMGATE BODI SVÃHÃ.' Gone, gone, everyone gone to the other shore, awakening. Or according to the Dalai Lama; 'Go, go, go beyond, go thoroughly beyond, and establish yourself in enlightenment.'

Swedish Words

CITRONFJÄRIL   The common brimstone butterfly.

ELVISP   Electric Whisk

HEMLÄNGTAN   A longing for home.

MORFAR   Mother's father.

MORMOR   Mother's mother.

OMPLANTERING   Transplantation, or re-planting.

SAFT   Cordial.

About the Author

James Tunney obtained an honours degree in law from Trinity College Dublin, qualified as a Barrister at the Honorable Society of the King's Inn, Dublin and obtained an LLM from Queen Mary College, University of London.

Since then he worked as a Lecturer and Senior Lecturer in UK universities. He has been a Visiting Professor in Germany and France, lecturer around the world and worked as an international legal consultant in places such as Lesotho and Moldova for bodies such as the UNDP. He talked in many countries and published regularly on issues associated with globalisation. He has taught, written and talked about subjects such as indigenous rights, travel and tourism law, culture and heritage, IP, communications technology law, competition law, China and World Trade.

He decided to leave the academic world behind to concentrate on artistic and spiritual development. He has exhibited paintings in a number of countries and has continued his writing.

In 2019 the following were published:

'Blue Lies September', a contemporary novel.

'The Mystical Accord – Sutras to Suit Our Times, Lines for Spiritual Evolution' a poetic work on mysticism.

'Konstnärernas Konstnär' (The Artist's Artist), an article on Strindberg in the Swedish annual 'Strindbergiana'.

CPSIA information can be obtained
at www.ICGtesting.com
Printed in the USA
LVHW031600180220
647329LV00002B/294